"Please don't run, Heather."

Michael watched Heather flinch. He'd said those words to her before, and on the steps of this very church. He'd gotten a face full of flowers—her wedding bouquet—the last time. This time he got much worse.

Heather turned and looked him straight in the eye. In that moment he saw unmasked all the hurt and disappointment she had carried with her all these years.

"Please, Heather." He came down one step, and then another, his hand extended. "Please stay. And then we can—"

What? Take up their lives where they left off? With her looking to the wrong people and places for happiness? And him, wishing she'd just once look at him, *really* look at him and see how much he loved her?

After the Storm:
A Kansas community unites to rebuild

Books by Annie Jones

Love Inspired

April in Bloom
Somebody's Baby
Somebody's Santa
Somebody's Hero
Marrying Minister Right

Steeple Hill Café

Sadie-in-Waiting
Mom Over Miami
The Sisterhood of the
   Queen Mamas

ANNIE JONES

Winner of the Holt Medallion for Southern Themed Fiction and the *Houston Chronicle*'s Best Christian Fiction Author of 1999, Annie Jones grew up in a family that loved to laugh, eat and talk—often all at the same time. They instilled in her the gift of sharing through words and humor, and the confidence to go after her heart's desire (and to act fast if she wanted the last chicken leg). A former social worker, she feels called to be a "voice for the voiceless" and has carried that calling into her writing by creating characters often overlooked in our fast-paced culture—from seventy-somethings who still have a zest for life to women over thirty with big mouths and hearts to match. Having moved thirteen times during her marriage, she is currently living in rural Kentucky with her husband and two children.

Marrying
Minister Right
Annie Jones

Steeple
Hill®

Published by Steeple Hill Books™

Special thanks and acknowledgment to
Annie Jones for her contribution to the
After the Storm miniseries

STEEPLE HILL BOOKS

Steeple
Hill®

Recycling programs
for this product may
not exist in your area.

ISBN-13: 978-0-373-81420-6

MARRYING MINISTER RIGHT

Printed in U.S.A.

Therefore put on the full armor of God,
so that when the day of evil comes, you may
be able to stand your ground, and after you have
done everything, to stand.

—*Ephesians* 6:13

Prologue

July 10
10:00 p.m.
Wichita, Kansas

"That's it! I am officially changing my name."

The old door to the main office of Helping Hands Christian Charity slammed, echoing through the darkened hallway. The charity's founder and longtime director pushed her straight light brown hair off her shoulders and stared at her name printed in gold on the frosted glass. "I am no longer Heather Waters."

Mary Kate Madison, her assistant, marched onward flicking off lights as she headed down the hallway. She raised her voice to be heard over the drone of the TV in the lobby, calling back, "Not this again."

"From this point on, I am going by what everybody and their dog seems to know me as." The thin soles of Heather's three-year-old, faux-leather bargain pumps kept a quick rhythm on the scuffed linoleum floor. "Heather Willya!"

"Did you say Heather Will You?" Mary Kate asked as she charged on ahead of her boss.

"Will*ya*," she corrected above the hum of the TV in the lobby. "As in Heather, will ya sign these forms? Heather, will ya see if you can find a few more dollars for this cause or that? Heather, will ya juggle your schedule to host an important meeting of the Interfaith Community Needs Assessment Council?"

"You love being counted on and we all know it." Mary Kate, who at twenty-three was five years younger than Heather but still tended to play mother hen, clucked her tongue as she reached the well-lit and finally vacant lobby. In the doorway she pivoted and held up her hand. "Oh, wait. Check the doors to make sure they're locked as you come down the hallway, if you don't mind, will you?"

"That's *Ms.* Willya to you!" Heather called back. She rattled a doorknob, found it secure and moved on. "All is as it should be. Everything is safe and secure and we can trust—"

"Hey, didn't you come from High Plains?" Mary Kate cut her off.

"High Plains?" Heather stopped in her tracks. "Why do you ask?"

Mary Kate pointed to the TV hung high in the lobby.

"An F3-level tornado devastated the small community of High Plains, Kansas, yesterday evening," the TV announcer was saying.

"What?" Heather stepped forward. She'd been so busy with work that she hadn't heard any news all day.

"The destruction is widespread," the announcer went on. "Emergency crews are on the scene. We are still waiting to see if there are any deaths or serious injuries."

Dead or injured? In High Plains? Heather staggered forward toward the small, flickering screen. A knot tightened in her stomach.

"You grew up there, right?" Her assistant looked from the broadcast to Heather then back to the broadcast.

"Yes, it's…" A place she had not visited or even so much as driven through since she had left it behind a decade ago. Heather couldn't imagine rubble where once had stood homes and businesses.

To her surprise, an aching sense of the familiar washed over her. The threat of tears blurred her vision. "It's *home.*"

All her life that was all she had wanted. A real home. Her mother tried so hard to make one for their family. But no amount of love and kindness on her part had made it happen. Nothing either of them did could make Heather's father love her.

"At present the town is using High

Plains Christian Church, which escaped virtually unscathed in the storm, as a base of operations."

The image of the simple old white church flashed on the screen and the world seemed to spin backward through time. Her cheeks flashed hot. Her knees wobbled for only a moment before she took a deep breath and shut her eyes to steady herself.

The day she left High Plains for good, never looking back, she was supposed to have been married in that very church. As long as she lived she would never forget opening the envelope in the sanctuary where she had spent so many joyous days of her life. In that envelope, delivered by a private investigator hired by her fiancé's family, she found a truth her mother had taken to her grave. Edward Waters was not her biological father.

And John Parker, son of the wealthiest family to ever live in High Plains, wanted nothing more to do with her. There would be no marriage. For only a moment

Heather had blamed the private investigator's report. But young as she was, she wasn't foolish enough to think that in this day and age someone would refuse to marry a person because of her lineage. No, Heather now understood why Edward Waters never would love her and that, despite his many youthful professions, John Parker had *never* really loved her.

Her world had fallen apart that day and she had crumbled with it. She had come so far since that wretched day. Yet this awful reminder of her hometown proved to her that she may have moved away, but she had not wholly moved on.

"Built in 1859, the church remains much as it did then, a beacon to those in need." The reporter spoke with a cultivated calm that belied the tragedy of the situation. "We interviewed the minister from the church earlier today and here's what he had to say."

Heather raised her hand to block the screen from her view. "I'll look this up online later tonight. It's just horrible but…it really doesn't have anything to do with me anymore. It's not like I even know anyone there any—"

Just then, between her splayed fingers, she caught a glimpse of a broad-shouldered man with wavy dark brown hair. He looked rumpled but in charge.

"Michael." Heather dropped her hand to her throat and fought to drag in a breath deep enough to allow her to speak above a dry, shocked whisper.

The years had treated him kindly. Given him fullness in the face and the beginning of lines fanning out from his startlingly blue eyes. Still, there was no mistaking him. "Michael Garrison."

"You know him?" Mary Kate's head whipped around.

The picture began to break up.

"I'm sorry," the news anchor came back. "We seem to have lost that connection. We'll go back to it after this message."

Heather exhaled slowly, her eyes on the TV where moments ago she had confronted her past. "Yeah, I know him. Or knew him. That is… I *thought* I knew him."

The Three Amigos. Everyone in town had called Michael, her and John Parker that from the time they had all been the lousiest players on a fairly lousy Little League team. They had formed a bond then—John, "Take-A-Hike Mike," so called because the only way he could get on base was to get hit by the ball and get a walk; and "Heather Duster." She threw herself into every base, trying too hard, wanting it too badly. Needing to prove she could do it, she would dive headlong, gritting her teeth and sliding with all her heart.

"You can never tell where Heather is standing until the dust settles," the coach would say.

From grade school through high school, nothing could separate the trio. Until one day during the summer between their junior and senior years. That was the summer that John Parker kissed Heather. Suddenly, three became a crowd. Michael hadn't seemed to mind; he wanted the best for his friends, he had said. He wanted them to be happy.

That's what he had *said.*

"So you *do* know him, or what?"

"I know him." Heather nodded, her eyes on the screen waiting to see if they would return to the story shortly. "The last time I saw the man, I threw my wedding bouquet in his face."

"You were going to *marry* him?" Mary Kate stabbed her finger at the TV.

"No, he was just—" A friend? A friend would never have done what Michael Garrison had done. In many ways, his role in what happened that day had hurt Heather more than John's. She knew why John couldn't go through with the marriage. Even though she still chafed at the way he had handled it, she had found a grudging respect for the fact that he hadn't gone forward with wedding vows he knew he could not honor for a lifetime. But Michael? Why had he gone along with it, allowed her public humiliation and done nothing to stop it? That, she could never understand. "Michael Garrison was just a—"

"Tell us, Reverend Garrison, what can

people watching do to help?" The news correspondent had come back on. He thrust the mic into the bleary-eyed, disheveled minister's face.

Such a good face. Heather could still see the kindness and commitment in the way he stood firm among the chaos and destruction. In the fact that he looked as though he had not rested since the storm had hit. In the fact that he was willing to speak on behalf of those who could not, at the moment, speak for themselves, with no regard for his own needs.

"Reverend Garrison," she murmured, shaking her head. Michael had always talked about entering the ministry, but she had never heard if he had actually followed through on that.

He stroked the stubby shadow of bristles along his jaw. When she had last seen him, he'd hardly been shaving at all. He had been so young then. They all had been.

"For the time being we have most of the basics covered," he said.

His hoarse voice tripped over her weary

nerves the way she imagined a thumb would strum over the taut strings of a guitar, leaving them vibrating. The news churned up a sudden clash of emotions, leaving her feeling raw.

"This is not something that will be a quick or easy fix." He shifted his weight. Tugged at his collar. Cleared his throat, clearly uncomfortable with the media attention. Still, he understood how important it was to get the message out, to speak for the people and the town he so loved. "We have a lot of damage, the full extent of which we still don't know. We have a fund set up through a local bank for contributions. So to anyone who wants to help that way, we'd appreciate it."

"Done," Heather said softly even as Mary Kate lunged for a pen and paper to jot down the information scrolling across the bottom of the screen.

"Should I write a request for a check from the board or send something from the floating fund?" Mary Kate asked above the scratching of her pen on the pad.

"Neither," Heather said. "I'll make a personal donation and solicit others on their behalf."

It was her calling to do for other people the things she had never been able to do for her own parents—give them a chance to heal their differences, to stay together and be a real family.

"And, of course, we could use your prayers," Michael concluded.

"Also done." Heather pressed her lips together, drew in a deep breath and finally looked away.

That was all she could do right now. Her father was ill; she couldn't leave town. Helping Hands Christian Charity was not designed, nor was it equipped, to rush in and give aid in emergency situations like this. She had an obligation to the people who donated to the organization to adhere to their mission. Still, she would do all she could personally to help the town she still loved, even if it had not seemed to love her back.

"Is there anything else you'd like to

say?" the reporter pressed on. "Anything more people can do to make a difference?"

For a second there was only silence.

Heather took the slip of paper from Mary Kate and did not look up. She did not need to see the man to know he was stroking his hand back through his hair, rubbing his chin and generally stalling for time. It was a habit he'd had since Little League. Always wanting to be sure he did and said the right thing, wanting to be conscious of other people's feelings. That was why, when he had completely disregarded her feelings on the biggest day of her life, it had wounded her so deeply.

She would send money to the town and certainly pray for all of them, but that was all she would do. All she *could* do.

"There is one more thing," Michael finally spoke up. "There are some tourist cottages by the river, a whole row of them."

Heather tensed.

"I, uh, I used to know the owner," Mike went on. "Well, uh, the owner's daughter, actually."

A shiver went down her spine.

"These cottages survived in pretty good shape. They aren't luxury accommodations by any means, but for families who have nowhere else to turn, who want to stay together in High Plains, they could become a real, if temporary, home."

"Home," she whispered again. She spun around and searched first the background of High Plains behind Michael, then the man's face. He had practically just spelled out Heather's personal mission statement. She fought back the tears for the second time tonight.

"If anyone knows how to get in touch with any member of the Waters family, or if any of them hear this interview…"

She could not go to High Plains herself right now. She could not send money from her charity without going through a time-consuming process. But she could do this. She could answer Michael Garrison's plea to help keep the families of High Plains together. She could grant permission on her father's behalf for the use of the cottages.

Doing so would mean that, at some point, she'd have to go back to that town to deal with the cottages in person. She shut her eyes. Would it really be so bad? She needed to check on her father and could easily let him know what she had done. He might not be happy with her acting on his behalf, but he hadn't been feeling well for some time. Nothing had been done with those cottages for so long, he would likely be glad to pass their responsibility on to her.

"Heather, will you help us out if you can?" Michael finally asked outright.

"Is he talking to you?" Mary Kate's eyes grew wide.

"Yes." He was talking to her. As an old friend. As a man of God. Perhaps even as a nudge from God. "Mary Kate, make the call and tell Michael Garrison they can use the cottages. I'll get it cleared through my father."

"What if he asks to speak to you?" Mary Kate had already picked up the handset, her hand hovering above the keypad on the phone.

"He had his chance to speak to me ten years ago and he kept quiet," she said softly.

"What? You really want me to tell him that?"

Heather blinked and came back to the present. "No. No, of course not. Tell him…" She looked out at her car next to Mary Kate's in the dark and otherwise empty parking lot. "Tell him I have a lot of personal and work-related issues colliding right now, but I will come to High Plains as soon as I can, to do whatever I can."

"When?" Mary Kate wanted to know.

Heather rubbed her eyes. They felt as though she had been in a sandstorm, tired, burning, as if they could use a good cry. She exhaled. Crying didn't accomplish anything. Action did. "Just tell him I'll be in High Plains when the dust settles. He'll understand."

With that she dug her cell phone from her bag to call her father, only then seeing multiple missed calls all from the same unknown number.

"Michael?" she whispered. Her pulse

thumped in her temples and her hand shook as she punched in the code to retrieve the first message. But it wasn't Michael.

"Ms. Waters, this is Galichia Heart Hospital. Your father was brought in a half hour ago. He's been asking us to get in touch with you. Please get back to us as soon as you can."

Chapter One

Dust. The Holy Bible tells us God created human life out of dust and that in time we would all return to it.

Almost a full month after the tornado had ripped through his town, Michael Garrison felt as if everything he owned, wore or ate was still covered with the stuff. Whole neighborhoods now seemed like little more than dump heaps and sandlots. In so many places the storm had stripped away not only grass and trees but also much of the topsoil. Some of the old-timers likened it to a small-scale dust bowl.

His scuffed and battered tennis shoes

kicked particles from the church's maroon-colored carpet even as he pushed the vacuum cleaner back and forth. The aging machine whirred loudly, practically wheezing and gasping for breath.

"Hang in there just a little longer, baby. We can't afford a new broom right now, much less a vacuum." He dragged it back across a spot he'd gone over…and over… and over before. "If you stay with me until we've got some sense of normalcy around here again…"

The engine sputtered.

"Yeah, you're probably right." He kicked the off switch at the base of the old-fashioned upright to turn the thing off. "Normalcy may be asking for way too much these days."

"You're talking to the vacuum cleaner now?" His niece, dressed in a lavender shirt and overalls, her light brown hair in braids, poked her head in the door. At just five foot one and wearing the deceptively sweet and modest outfit that she had complained about all morning, she looked even younger than her fourteen years.

Michael squeezed his eyes shut and raised his head to call back to her, "Talking to inanimate objects gives me practice for talking to people who never listen. Like my niece, whom I asked to go to the store to get us sodas about three minutes ago."

"I'm going, I'm going, all right? I just—"

"Whatever they have will be fine." He cut her off before she could launch into another list of excuses why she shouldn't have to go out in the heat. "Or if you want to stay here, you can vacuum and I'll go get us something cold to drink."

"Vacuum? With that antique?" She crinkled up her nose. "My mom never makes me do that stuff. I don't even know how. Besides, I think that thing is actually making the carpet dirtier."

"Don't you listen to her, old girl." He patted the bulging cloth bag on the old upright and was rewarded with a cloud of ultrafine powdery dust.

Avery laughed.

He liked hearing her laugh. She'd had a hard year and didn't laugh nearly as much as he thought a kid her age should. So he played up the scene for her enjoyment, waving his hands, pretending to stagger around unable to see, coughing.

More girlish laughter.

Spinning around, he grinned to himself. Sunlight streamed in around him. The play of shadows and light against one another made a spotlight in which specks and dots sparkled.

"I'll be back when the dust settles." The message Heather Waters had sent echoed in his thoughts again, as it had many times in the last four weeks.

He watched the residue drip and drift and glitter in the sunbeam for a moment. He gritted his teeth to stave off the pangs of unresolved emotions twisting in his gut. If Heather held true to her word, he might never see her again.

Hadn't he resigned himself to that fate ten years ago? He had kept his thoughts and feelings to himself, wanting only her happiness, when the only girl he had ever really loved wanted to marry John Parker. And then when that girl had fled from this church, hurt and humiliated by John leaving her at the altar, he had let her go because it was best for her and, in the long run, for him.

Now he had to do that again. He had too much work to do, too many people counting on him to allow himself the luxury of being distracted by something that could never be.

"Okay, how about I go for sodas and you do something else to pitch in around here?" He wasn't letting the girl slip free of taking some responsibility for basic chores.

"I said I'd get the sodas." She gave a huff.

Michael tugged free the hem of the well-worn multicolored T-shirt he had pulled from the pile of donated clothes. He'd tried to make sure Avery had clean laundry, but neglected to do the same for himself. He wiped his brow, then took a moment to look over the sanctuary.

It was a simple design. High, wooden

ceilings with sturdy support beams arching upward. The style, he'd always been told, was meant to mimic the inside of a boat to remind them always that they were to be fishers of men.

He studied the long, tall, stained-glass windows, glowing in shades of red, blue, yellow and purple. Years ago their insurance company had required them to be encased in protective safety glass. That and the sturdy boat-bottom design had protected the sanctuary from all but cosmetic damage.

But not from dust and dirt and even trash that still blew through the streets and gathered like fallen leaves in corners and along curbs all over town.

"And I will get the sodas, if you want me to or whatever, but…" Avery launched into yet another excuse for her not having done as she was asked.

"No." Michael sighed and rubbed his hand over his face. "I'll go. Why don't you—"

"Why don't you tell me why you didn't go when I asked, Avery?" She spoke in a low voice, a booming imitation of him with one thumb hooked in the strap of her overalls.

In the next moment, she turned her shoulders, folded her hands in front of her and spoke in a soft, sweet voice. "I'm trying, Uncle Michael. Why won't you listen to me?"

Back to the imitation of him, she blustered, "That's because I'm a big grump like I've been all week, Avery. In fact, I'm so grumpy lately I've had to resort to talking to my cleaning supplies."

"Says the girl talking to *herself*," Michael muttered, even as he chuckled softly and began rolling the cord of the vacuum. "Guess we're all on edge a little lately. Kind of in a transition period, not really sure what to do or what will happen next."

"Well, maybe the person who's looking around out here can help with that." Avery pushed the door open and stood back.

"Heather?" Michael took a step forward.

"Wow. You do have dust in your eyes if

you think…" Avery looked at him slyly. "Hey, that's who you *wish* it was, isn't it?"

"No, no. She wouldn't… I don't have any reason to…" He looked up at the altar and sighed. "Yes. Yes, I've sort of been keeping an eye out for her to come back."

Avery rolled her eyes the way young girls do at someone old, in this case twenty-eight years old, like Michael. She clearly thought him totally inept when it came to relationships with members of the opposite sex. "Well, until she does—"

"Yeah, I know." Michael put his hand up to forestall some cutting remark from the girl. His sister, Avery's mom, had struggled with the girl always having a flip answer for everything. Michael hoped to defuse that a bit by taking the fun and shock value out of her smart comebacks by beating her to the punch line. "Until Heather comes back I can always talk to my vacuum cleaner."

"I was going to say you should talk to this guy who's been hanging around the lobby the last few minutes."

"Oh. Uh…a guy, huh?" Michael cleared his throat. He really wished he had that cold drink right now. "Who is he? What does he want?"

"Reverend Garrison?" A man who looked like he saw the world through numbers on the other side of thick but new glasses, barged in past Avery.

Michael came down the aisle and shook his hand. "Michael Garrison."

"Paisley," he said.

Michael glanced down at his grubby shirt and jeans. "Tie-dyed, actually."

"No, my *name* is Paisley. I'm here for the…the…" He reared back as if to give out with a great, whooshing sneeze.

Michael stepped back.

Nothing happened. The man cleared his throat and finished. "Temp job."

"Temp?" Michael shook his head. "I don't know who gave the idea that we're hiring, even on a temp basis, but—"

"No, no. I'm an intake worker for a social service agency in Manhattan, and they are loaning me out for a few days. I was supposed to meet someone with a private organization looking for a place to set up a base of operations."

"Not anyone from our church," Michael assured him.

"Is it a *lady* someone?" Avery came into the sanctuary, took a seat in the last row, leaned both elbows on the pew in front of her and rested her chin in her hands.

"Yes, actually it is." He squinted at Avery as if sizing her up. "I got to town early so I've been going around to places I thought she might go. It's a Christian charity so I thought, you know, churches." He sort of wrinkled his nose as he said it.

Michael didn't know if the man was showing contempt or felt another sneeze coming on.

"Ask him," Avery mouthed as she pointed to the man heading for the door.

Michael shook his head. Avery was trying to make more out of this than it merited. Besides, Michael didn't want to know if Heather was in town or not. It didn't matter either way. He had his work to do and she had hers.

Mr. Paisley reached the door, paused and looked up.

This time to emphasize the urgency of her silent demand, Avery stood and gestured with both hands. Michael replied with his own emphatic gesture, slashing his hand across his throat to tell her to cut it out. He shook his head again.

The door creaked open.

"Heather Waters," Avery shouted just as the man crossed the threshold into the lobby.

"What?" He caught the door before it could swing shut and stared at the teen.

In a frantic, full-body gesture, Michael swung his arms out, brought them in across his body, then out again as though trying to signal an oncoming train to hit the brakes.

"The, um, *someone* you're looking for?" Avery glanced Michael's way, rolled her eyes and totally ignored his wishes. "Is her name Heather Waters?"

"Yes. Yes, it is. Do either of you have any idea how I can find her here in town?"

Heather. In town.

Michael dropped his hands to his sides. "No. I have no idea where she is. I doubt she'd seek me out."

"But he wants her to!" Avery called out even as the man nodded and went back out the door.

"Avery, that's enough," Michael snapped.

"What's the big deal? You're single. My mom always says, 'Michael's a minister, he's not a monk.' She says she wishes you'd find a nice girl but you're too hung up on some girl who…" The girl's jaw dropped. She jumped up from the pew so fast she knocked a hymnal from the rack. "No way!"

"I said that's enough." He had dealt with far too much chaos these last few weeks. He did not need any more of it in his life, especially from an already-hard-to-handle teenager with a gleam in her eye and an impossible matchmaking scheme churning in her mind.

"But…but she's the girl, *isn't she?*" Avery pointed to the door. "You should go.

She's in town somewhere! You should go and find her and tell her—"

"She doesn't want to hear anything from me." Though Michael wasn't sure why Heather felt the way she did, she had made herself perfectly clear. Michael had never wanted anything for Heather but her happiness.

If talking to him, or even just seeing him brought back old feelings that caused her pain, then Michael would do everything in his power to honor her wishes and make himself scarce around her.

"But if she needs a building as a base, maybe she could work out of the church. Then the two of you could—"

"There is no two of us. Don't you get that, Avery?" He raised his voice to his niece in the house of the Lord. If just talking about Heather Waters did this to him, he was better off avoiding her anyway.

He clenched his jaw, then eased his breath out slowly. "I'm sorry. I… You were right when you said I've been really grumpy lately."

"No problem," she said quietly. But a quiet born of anger, embarrassment, injured feelings, not respect.

Not good, Michael thought. He had made so much progress bringing Avery out of her surly shell and now he had all but shoved her right back into it.

"Avery, I—"

"What did you want me to do around here?" She bent and picked up the hymnal and all but jammed it back in the rack.

"You can stay and go around the building picking up whatever the wind has blown in or…" He hesitated to send her out on a snack run now. One of her mother's concerns was that as her defiance grew she'd decide to strike out on her own, or take off with some of her more questionable friends. "Or just put the vacuum away and make a couple of sandwiches in the church kitchen."

She folded her arms and narrowed her eyes. "What? Am I grounded?"

Suddenly, even having her take the shortcut through the parking lot to the small parsonage felt risky. "No. You're not grounded. I just think…" That he was in over his head dealing with a mouthy young teen with raging hormones and authority issues. "Look, just stay in the church while I go get us some sodas. Answer the phone. Take messages. I won't be gone long."

"Take your time. I'm not going anywhere." She turned, went to the door in a sulky huff, then looked back over her shoulder, and through clenched teeth added, "Ever."

The door swung open and shut.

A burst of wind stirred the grit-filled air.

Michael shut his eyes intending to send up a prayer dart, a quick, focused plea for…

He needed guidance about Avery. He needed clear views and insight and the sort of inner peace that only comes from quiet contemplation. He needed to find a way to put the woman who had held his heart for more than a decade out of his thoughts for good.

"I need a cold soda," he muttered. He opened his eyes and took a step, bumping into the old vacuum. Dust flew, dancing in the sunlight once more and leaving a film on his arms, shirt and jeans.

Life, Michael reminded himself, came from the dust. Which seemed very appropriate, because at the moment he felt like dirt.

Chapter Two

"You are the only person I know who takes time off from work to do some more work."

"I'm not staying in High Plains. I have hotel reservations in Kansas City that they will only hold until 6:00 p.m. By tomorrow I'll be shopping on the Plaza. Today I'm just stopping in for a few hours, maybe half a day, to check on the cabins. They are my responsibility now, you know." Heather kept both hands on the steering wheel of the SUV that had come to her after her father's death. She tried to keep talking and driving to a minimum but today she welcomed the company, though she could have done with a little less static from Mary Kate in her earpiece.

"Your dad has only been gone a few weeks, Heather." Mary Kate seemed to need to remind Heather. "After all those days shuttling between work and caring for him in the hospital, you've had almost no time to grieve."

"We each grieve in our own way, in our own time." Heather had been grieving the absence of Edward Waters almost her entire life. In their last few days together, they had reached a resolution that was at least satisfying. Edward had let her know how much he appreciated her visits and she had thanked him for providing for her so comfortably as a child and for leaving her the bulk of his estate, including the cottages in High Plains. "I'll have plenty of time for…for myself once I get the temporary intake worker set up here. I left High Plains a long time ago. There's nothing to keep me here even a few hours longer than necessary."

She went gliding past the cottages. Since

she had agreed to meet the intake worker in town, she did not stop at her property. Though they had really begun to show their age, the cottages looked pretty good at first glance. Needed paint and some cosmetic shoring up, clearing away of dead brush, but otherwise, not bad.

As always the river that lay beyond them wound on in a swift, constant current. It served to remind her that life went on. God's eye was on every living thing and even when things seemed out of control, He was always in charge. His will, His plan remained steadfast.

"Nothing for you in High Plains?" Mary Kate asked. "Are you sure? Not even that cutie-pie of a minister?"

Heather clenched her jaw and stared at the road. "I have no intention of even seeing Michael Garrison. Trust me."

"Wow, Heather." Without a tsk or a tut or a cluck, just a subtle shift in the tone of her voice, Mary Kate slid into mother-hen mode. "Isn't it awfully hard to drive that way?"

Heather leaned forward, squinting at the

horizon, not-letting her assistant's attitude intrude on the moment as she scanned the once-familiar road. She should have seen the first signs of High Plains by now. But all she saw was dirt—trash blowing about and the occasional downed tree.

Finally, she sighed, showing her impatience with her own faltering memory, which must have all but rewritten the landscape around her. She asked, "Drive what way?"

"With that big ol' chip on your shoulder?"

"I don't… I didn't… You don't understand. Michael was my friend since…"

She passed the spot where a sign that welcomed people to High Plains had once stood and saw only two posts thrusting up out of a concrete base. The posts were twisted and bent like the gnarled branches of a long-dead tree.

She was at the edge of town, where Main Street should have been populated with well-kept buildings and neatly groomed sidewalks. She turned her head to look at the park that lay between the cottages and the Old Town Hall.

Heather took her foot off the gas pedal as the realization hit her. It was not her memory that had faded. She *was* seeing the first signs of High Plains, of what was left of High Plains. "Oh, Mary Kate. It's gone."

"The chip?"

"The town." Heather managed only a whisper as she scanned the space from where the gazebo used to stand to the bare spot where the Old Town Hall, a symbol of the very heart of the community, had once stood. "I have to go, Mary Kate. I'll call you later."

If her assistant protested, Heather did not know. She took the earpiece off and tossed it onto the seat next to her.

She looked at the rubble, then toward the town stretched out along Main Street ahead of her. Here and there something remained seemingly untouched. Trash and leaves blew about, the empty sidewalks giving the place a sense of being neglected and abandoned.

She had thought she was prepared for what she would find, but she had not counted on the potent mix of sparseness and destruction and her own muddled emotions. Her eyes stung. She willed herself to stay strong and calm.

Never let them see you cry.

Tears did not change things. They had not made her father love her and they did not inspire confidence in people looking for reassurance in times of turmoil. These people had gone through enough without a weepy former local showing up and adding to it. She had to focus. She had to fix her mind on what had brought her here.

She lifted her eyes and caught a glimpse of High Plains Christian Church at the end of Main Street. Aside from a few odd-colored shingles, the obvious sign of patching on the roof, it looked just as it had that summer day ten years ago when she had run off and left…

"Michael?"

Loss and embarrassment, feelings she could not define and the memory of a happiness she had long forgotten came crashing in on Heather at just seeing Michael Garrison again.

She let the car roll to a stop as she concentrated on the lone figure walking along Main Street toward the church. If she had not seen him on the news the day after the twister, Heather doubted she would ever have imagined that the tall, broad-shouldered man in faded jeans and a tie-dyed T-shirt could be the same kid who had taught her not to be afraid of a pop fly. Or the skinny teenager who had allowed her to be like a member of his family and thus learn the importance of one. She certainly wouldn't have guessed it was the young man she had smacked in the face with a wedding bouquet.

Still a block away from the church, she watched the man in front pause and look up toward the steeple. Sunlight tipped his dark brown hair in golden highlights. He lifted his hand, the one not holding two cans of soda, to shade his face. He stood there a moment as if gathering strength. But for what?

Heather needed only to glance around her to have her answer. Michael Garrison loved High Plains. He loved his family, who had built so much of the town. She did not doubt that he loved his congregation. Right now, all the people Michael loved were trying to come to terms with the agony and confusion in the aftermath of this catastrophe. Of course the man needed strength.

What a blessing that he knew he could find it—from the Lord, first, but also from the town, from his family, from his congregation and from…

"Me." Heather could all but see how Mary Kate would give her best "What am I going to do with you?" head shake at that. She didn't care. She had come to High Plains to see if she could help, if there was anyone in need.

And she saw a need in Michael.

She directed the heavy SUV up the street. The sound of small rocks, twigs and debris crunching under the tires must have alerted Michael, because he turned and squinted in her direction. He did not seem to recognize her.

Butterflies dipped and dove in her stomach. She bit her lower lip to contain her smile at having the upper hand on her old friend. Her ex-friend, she corrected herself.

She took a deep breath and considered stepping on the gas and not slowing down, much less stopping. But when she got close enough to see his face, so warm and ready to greet whoever had come into his town, she let down her guard…and rolled down the window.

"Need a lift or you plan on staying true to your old nickname, Take-A-Hike Mike?"

"Take-A…" He squinted, stepped toward the SUV, then broke into a broad grin. "Heather? Heather Duster? Is that you?"

"I told you I'd be here when the dust settled." She hit the electric door lock and it popped up. "Hop in."

"I'm just going over to the church. Just about to grab a sandwich for lunch." He gestured with the soda cans clasped in his strong grasp. "Hey, you should join us."

"Us?" The single-syllable word hit Heather like a slap in the face. It had never dawned on Heather that Michael might be a part of an *us* now.

"My niece has been staying with me this summer. Avery? You remember Avery, don't you?"

"Remember her?" Heather relaxed, though for the life of her she couldn't imagine why thinking that Michael Garrison had a significant other in his life would make her tense. She laughed and scooted toward the passenger side to better talk to him. "I helped you babysit her when she was little. In fact, I drove you to your sister's to do it because you didn't have a car."

"I was saving money for college. Besides, who needed a car when one of your best friends got the latest model for her sixteenth birthday?"

Heather ran her hand along the leather dashboard of the new SUV that had come to her as part of her inheritance and said softly, "A car was always easier to give than affection."

Michael folded his arms on the open window and leaned in, all concern and kindness. "How is your father?"

"He died two weeks ago." She hung her head for only a moment before looking at Michael again. "That's why I couldn't get to High Plains until now."

"Heather, I am so sorry." He reached out to her.

"It's not…" She looked down at where his tanned and rugged hand grasped the pale, soft skin of her arm. His calluses and scars bore evidence of the kind of work he had been doing, that he had put his time, his effort, his very body out there to serve others. It humbled her, knowing she had spent most of the last year fund-raising, doing paperwork and dealing with her father's last days as if it were just another item on her already crowded to-do list. The contrast struck her in more ways than one. "I appreciate your sympathy but I'm all right."

"That's good to know. Now tell me, are *we* all right?"

"We?" She looked up into his eyes.

They were still blue. So very blue. In them shone depths of hope and faith and gentleness that Heather had never seen before.

She flexed her fingers and pursed her lips. Tell him you forgive him, her mind urged. But her mouth could not seem to form the words. She had trusted him more than she had ever trusted anyone in her whole life. "Michael, I think you should know I'm only here for—"

"I just can't work in this—" a man interjected, wiping his nose "—environment."

"Hey, Mr. Paisley!" Michael stepped back and held his hand out to indicate Heather. "This is the lady you were looking for."

"Good! I...I...I quit!" He coughed, then gave a wave to Heather through the window. "I'm sorry, Ms. Waters, but I have allergies and that...that...that young lady..."

"Avery?" Michael frowned. "Avery did something to you?"

"I don't want to get anyone in trouble, but..." Paisley coughed then kept moving past them, calling after himself. "But I think that before you turn that young lady loose in your church with a vacuum again, you probably should instruct her that the dust is supposed to go into the bag, not spew out of it."

"She was probably trying to help," Michael said to Heather through slightly clenched teeth.

"But you can't quit…if you run off *I'll* have to…" Heather pushed open the passenger door and leaned out to call after the man, who was already fumbling to get into a small car parked at an odd angle along the devastated remnants of the street.

He got in and slammed the door. The engine started.

"Stay myself," she murmured even as the man waved again and pulled away.

"Sorry about that." Michael peered at her through the lowered window of the opened passenger door. He scratched his scalp, his head lowered just enough to hide his full expression, then his gaze flicked upward, finding her. His lips twitched. He did not look one bit sorry at all. "I'd have offered to run him down and tackle him. Get him in a hammerlock or…uh…throw a monkey wrench at him or…uh, give him a proper Bible thumping, but I don't think it would have mattered."

Heather sighed. She could make a joke about his poor athletic prowess but she just didn't feel like laughing right now. She felt like…

She met Michael's gaze.

Her breath caught in the back of her throat. Despite the August heat, her skin drew into a million tiny tingle bumps. She had no idea what that feeling winding around inside her was. Fear? Anger? Frustration? Joy?

Heather put her chilled fingertips against her collarbone and pressed her lips together. She could not identify her own reaction, but she did know that she was in a bind. Her temp worker had flaked out and it would take at least a couple of days to get a new one in.

"It's good to see you, Heather. I really didn't think you'd come back."

She hadn't. Not to stay.

"I have reservations at a hotel that…" She just could not finish that sentence. She could not look at the devastation in High Plains or face the dedication in Michael's eyes and announce her intentions to go shopping on the Plaza.

Good and bad, this town and its people had given her her start. Couldn't she give them twenty-four hours of her long-overdue time off?

The church's bells rang out, making Michael jump. She supposed if he'd been another kind of man he'd have cussed a blue streak. Instead, he winced and ducked his head, his eyes scrunched shut.

"Problem?" she had to ask.

"Always." He opened his eyes and fixed his gaze on her as though nothing else in the world mattered. "But the good news in all this is that it's brought an old friend back. I could sure use a friend right now. That's gotta make things better, right?"

Decision time. Leave and put the town and Michael behind her. Or stay and take a chance at putting the past behind her and getting on with her life.

I need a friend right now. The sincerity of his words got to her. This wasn't just another job for her charity, not just another case. This was her hometown. This was a man who had once been her teammate, her confidant, her friend.

"I don't know if it will make things better, Michael, but I am here for the time being." She could not promise to mend their friendship or anything more than this: "And I'll stay until I can hire another worker to represent Helping Hands. I'll do whatever I can for the town."

"Great."

The clanging bells interrupted them again. Michael jerked his head toward the church. "Let's start by dealing with those bells."

"It's not an emergency, is it?" she asked over the slamming passenger door. "I assumed they were on a timer. Just a normal part of life here."

"Then you assumed too much, my friend. There is no normal life around here these days. But I don't think for a minute it's a real emergency. At least not until I get my hands on that niece of mine."

Chapter Three

When they reached the church, Michael dashed up the front stairs, taking them two at a time in his rush to get to his niece. Or maybe he did it, just a little, to show Heather that he wasn't still that ungainly, hesitant kid she had once known.

Heather held back. She gave a quick glance in the direction of the river then down the street. "Maybe I should leave you to this while I go see how things are at the cottages."

The bells stopped ringing.

Heather backed away.

"What? No." Michael followed her lead,

retracing his path until he had gone half-way back down the stairs. "Please, don't run off."

He'd said those words to her before, and on the steps of this very church. Then he'd gotten a face full of flowers. This time he got much worse.

Heather turned and looked him straight in the eye. In that moment he saw unmasked all the hurt and disappointment she had carried with her all these years.

For an instant his attention was divided. But only for a second. Many times a day Avery pulled something to demand his attention and he gave it to her. Heather, on the other hand, had stayed out of his life for far too long for him to simply let her slip away again.

"Please, Heather." He came down one step and then another, his hand extended. "Please stay. This won't take long and then we can—"

What? Take up their lives where they left off? With her turning to the wrong people and places for happiness? And him wishing she'd just once look at him, *really* look at him and see how much he loved her?

"Just…come inside. We'll…take things from there," he said softly.

Her whole body went straight and stiff. Her hands balled into fists at her sides. She tipped her head to one side and her hair swept over her shoulders.

Anxious. Uncertain. Agitated. Distressed.

Someone else might have used those kinds of words to describe how she looked just then. If asked, Michael would have said she looked…

"Amazing," he muttered.

"What?" She tilted her head back and narrowed her eyes against the brightness of the August sun.

"To see you here after all this time. To have you back in High Plains and here at the church." He took his eyes off her just long enough to glance up at the church doors, trying to urge her to come with him. "It's pretty amazing, don't you think?"

"Not exactly the word I'd use." She shook her head then shut her eyes.

"Besides, being at the church isn't the same as… I don't want to go in the sanctuary, Michael."

"You what?"

"It's silly, I know, after all these years." She lifted her chin and met his gaze at last. "But I'm just not ready."

"Okay. That's okay. There's no reason to go in the sanctuary now. The bells are controlled by a computer in the room right off the choir loft." He stepped down again, his hand still out to her. "Of course if you don't get over this anxiety by Sunday, you'll miss out on hearing me preach."

He wanted her to hear him preach. The thought was as close to vanity as Michael had ever had. He wanted the girl he had loved for so long, whom he would always love, to hear him do what God had called him to do.

"I won't be here Sunday," she said flatly.

Michael lowered his hand. "Oh."

"But if you really want me to stay now, I guess I can come in and look around." She gazed toward the cottages, her shoulders rose then fell and she turned to him and gave him a crooked smile. "I don't suppose you have a place where I can set up a temporary office for my charity?"

"I don't know what you'll need, but feel free to see if there's enough unoccupied space in the basement." So maybe she wouldn't stick around long enough to see him in the pulpit. Still, he had made a breakthrough.

He spread his hand on the wind-battered paint of the church's outer door and pushed it open.

She followed him up the stairs, tucking a strand of her long hair delicately behind her ear as she looked down at her feet.

He grinned so broadly it actually made his cheeks ache, unable to take his eyes off her even as he held the door open. She passed through and he hurried forward to lead the way.

The walls around Heather Waters's heart might not have come tumbling down but they had cracked. If she spent the day with him, he could show just how sorry he was for whatever he had done to hurt her. He could prove to her that he was a better man than the awkward, fumbling kid who—

"Oof!" The handle of the old vacuum gouged him right in the gut seconds before his momentum carried him headfirst over the mangy old thing.

His arms flailed. The soda cans slipped from his grasp. He kicked his leg to try to regain his balance. Bad idea.

His borrowed T-shirt ripped. One can of soda rolled off down the steps. The other bounced off the wall and began spewing a stream of foam high into the air. Michael took a full face-plant into the ever-filthy-from-the-tornado-aftermath carpet.

"Michael, are you all right?" Heather rushed toward him, her hands outstretched.

He was fine. Or as fine as any man could be under the circumstances. Still, he thought of groaning and playing up the injured angle in hopes that Heather might cradle his head in her lap, stroke his hair and tell him—

"It worked! I wasn't sure it would, but look, here you are. It really worked!"

Michael looked up to find Avery standing over him, beaming with pure adolescent pride.

"What worked?" He pushed himself up to his elbows, then to a sitting position, then, clumsily and reluctantly, to his feet. He smacked dust from his shirt and grumbled. "Don't tell me you set the vacuum cleaner—the vacuum I asked you to put away for me—here, then rang the bells knowing I'd come running and trip over it?"

"No." She hesitated and Michael couldn't read if that was because she was lying or because she was secretly wishing she had thought of a plan that clever. "Mr. Paisley had some kind of attack or something. He was coughing and saying he couldn't breathe and he ran out the door."

"Yeah, we already heard about you and Mr. Paisley and your attempt at reverse vacuum cleaning." Michael considered giving the old vacuum a kick for emphasis but reined in the impulse in favor of showing Avery, and Heather, his calm, even-tempered, mature side.

"I didn't attempt to *clean* anything." Avery sneered. "I was putting the thing away. Like *you* told me to."

"Oh, so that man's choking and gasping was actually *my* fault?" Michael looked down, first at his tattered shirt then at the soda-soaked carpet and shook his head. "And the bell ringing? Am I accountable for *that*, too?"

"Well, if you'd gotten back with the drinks sooner…" She made a face. "Of course, now we don't have any drinks at all." She heaved a sigh. "Anyway, I figured somebody needed to know that that Paisley guy had hit the road so I rang the bells because I knew you'd come. You always come when there's something that needs to be done, Uncle Michael. Even if what needs to be done is yelling at me! Especially if it's yelling at me!"

Michael froze, his head still down, and chided himself for not putting it all together more quickly. What Avery had done, knowingly putting herself at risk of getting in trouble to help someone else, was, in its own odd way, a selfless act. Hardly the kind of thing the kid would have done just a few weeks ago. "Wow, Avery."

"Wow, that was good, or wow, that was dumb?" she asked, her nose crinkled.

Before he could answer that, Heather stepped up and pitched in, righting the old vacuum as she gave Avery a nod of approval and said, "I think what you did was pretty ingenious."

"Hear that, Uncle Michael?" The kid puffed out her chest and hooked her thumb in her overall strap again. "I'm a genius! Guess it runs in the family, huh?"

"Actually?" He stuck his fingers through the big hole torn in his loaner T-shirt and wriggled them. "I reacted kind of like a dope. Maybe genius is the kind of thing that skips a generation."

"Like athletic ability?" Heather gave him a friendly nudge in the back before she turned her attention on Avery. "Your uncle never could get out of the way of anything. Not even a slow, high-arching softball thrown by a ten-year-old. He was clearly out of his league with this piece of sophisticated machinery."

"That was then." Michael pushed the vacuum against the wall then turned to face the pair so happy to give him good-natured grief. "This is—"

"Now let me get this straight." Avery waved her hand to cut Michael off and focused her whole bright expression on Heather. "You knew Uncle Michael when… Hey! Are you *her?*"

"Her? Her, who?" Heather put her hands on her hips and planted herself between Avery and Michael. "Should I know what you're talking about? Or rather, *who* you're talking about?"

"*The* girl." Avery said it in a way that only a young teen could. In a world-weary, acerbic tone, implying that it was so obvious she was embarrassed at having to articulate it even in this small way for him.

"That's enough, Avery." Mortified, Michael nabbed his niece gently but firmly by the arm and spun her around to point her toward the stairs that led to the basement. "Why don't you go make lunch, as I asked before?"

"The more you try to get me out of the way, the more you might as well blast it from the bell tower yourself." Avery did not budge. "This is the girl."

Had he always been this conspicuous in his love for Heather? Suddenly he wondered if she had known all along and secretly felt sorry for him. Maybe that was why she had stayed away. Maybe that was why she seemed so reluctant to hang around now.

His throat closed up at the idea. He wanted more than ever to move Avery along to keep her from making this worse.

"This is *a* girl," Michael said, still trying to get Avery to give up and go.

"Excuse me." Heather put her hand on Michael's arm, her expression confused but confident. "In case you haven't noticed, I'm a woman now, not a girl."

His gaze dipped to her hand. He wondered if she could feel how his pulse had suddenly picked up or if she read anything into the way his voice went deep and dry as he whispered, "I noticed."

"Whoo-hoo. Uncle Michael's girl is right here in High Plains! She's right here in our church."

"Go make yourself a sandwich, Avery." He couldn't exactly scold her, could he? She'd been obnoxious, but in the goofiest and sweetest of ways, and all out of love. Hard to punish that, and especially not with that precious phrase still lingering in the air. *Our* church. She'd called High Plains Christian Church *our* church. Pride welled up inside him. He gave the young girl who had been put in his care a wink and a grin as he said, "Make one for me and my *friend,* too, please."

"Friend? Oh, right. *Friend.*" Avery gave her own exaggerated wink, then headed for the basement stairs with a sway and a swagger to her step. "She's a girl. And a friend. But she's not a girlfriend. Oh, no. *Not* a girlfriend."

Heather watched the girl, then turned to

Michael with a look that told him she had no idea what had just happened.

"Don't pay any attention to Avery. She's at that age…" He craned his neck to call out after his niece. "The age when she would practically have a stroke from embarrassment if her old uncle showed up to say hi to her Sunday night Youth Group meeting wearing those orange sweatpants he found in the donation bin, a purple K-State T-shirt and those green plastic garden clogs that the housekeeper left in the parsonage when she moved out last week."

"Couldn't be any worse than what you have on now!" The girl disappeared from sight.

He chuckled softly then gave Heather a shrug. "Believe it or not, that wasn't so bad, all in all. Her folks sent her here to get her away from some bad influences and break some troubling habits. Couple of months ago? That exchange would have been filled with disrespect and more than a few dirty words."

She nodded.

He held his hand out toward the basement steps. "Let's look around and see if we can find a place for you to use for your charity before Avery serves up sandwiches and more grief for me."

"Clearly, she gets a kick out of giving you a hard time." Heather dipped her chin and looked at him slyly. "I seem to recall that was a favorite pastime of a certain young girl we both knew, as well."

"And the woman that young girl grew into?" He cocked one shoulder back, laced his arms, recently buffed up from doing so much manual labor, over his chest and narrowed his eyes at her.

"She…she thinks you've had a hard enough time the last month." Heather smiled, though there was sadness in that smile, and moved past him to head downstairs. "Though if you insist on wearing that tie-dyed shirt with the big hole in it, I may not be able to keep my thoughts to myself."

"Little too risqué for a minister, huh?" He pulled the shirt out and up slightly so he could better examine the damage.

"A minister," she repeated quietly. "That's just... I'm so...happy for you."

She didn't sound happy. She sounded as though she couldn't quite believe he had the right stuff for the job. He took a deep breath and decided to let it go. "Let's see if there's a spot in the basement that will do for your work."

Because they had classrooms upstairs, the church basement had remained uncluttered except for the day care. That had made it the ideal spot for a makeshift headquarters after that awful night in July when so many had lost so much.

"You remember that this is the auditorium/gymnasium." Michael pointed to the huge room directly across from the kitchen. He flicked on the light to reveal the stage at one end and a basketball hoop at the other. "We used it for emergency shelter those first few days. Now it's just the lost and found."

"Your congregation must be terribly absentminded," she joked, gesturing toward the tables full of odds and ends under the basketball hoop.

"The lost and found for the whole town," he clarified. "We needed one place to bring things that people find that might be important and a place for anyone missing things to come to see if they'd been found."

"There's still a lot of stuff even now," she said. "I'd have thought people would have gathered up pretty much all they were going to find by now, though."

"Not by a long shot. The tornado carried some things miles from their homes." He held out his hand to guide her toward the stage end of the gym. "Every chance they get, people are out searching for things they want desperately to recover. Avery and I were just out paying a call on Jesse Logan at the Circle L Ranch. He's a great guy with some serious stuff going on. We tried to help find his family's heirloom diamond engagement ring, but it has yet to be recovered."

"Engagement ring?" she murmured even as she bowed her head and folded her right hand over her left, hiding the spot where she had once hoped to wear John Parker's wedding ring.

He didn't know if it was his training as a minister to have a sensitivity to the things people did as much as they said or his long history with Heather that made him notice that. "It's not just that it's a family heirloom. Jesse's wife was killed in the tornado."

"Oh, no. Michael, that's so awful." Her concern was clear in her beautiful eyes.

That made him feel that she should hear the whole story, to put it in perspective and because maybe she could think of something to do to help. "Marie, Jesse's wife, had left the engagement ring with her wedding ring and a letter on the day of the storms. She took off, intending to leave him and abandon their newborn babies."

"Babies?" she whispered.

"Triplets. Born prematurely," he confirmed. "So the whole town has been pitching in to look for that ring. It means a lot more to him than a just a piece of jewelry. It's been in the Logan family for generations, since our town's founding."

She looked back at the lost-and-found

tables and smiled weakly. "It's a good town, Michael. Good people."

"I didn't think you remembered that."

"I did. I do. That's why I want to try to help, if I can. I have to follow the mandates of my organization. I can't just commit our resources to something because it's dear to my heart."

"I understand. Maybe I'd be of more service if you'd tell me just what these mandates are." He led her out of the gym.

She walked beside him down the hallway, her demeanor that of an impassioned professional as she told him, "The mission of Helping Hands Christian Charity is to keep families in crisis together. A lot of times when things go awry, kids get sent to other relatives or even go into the foster care system. Parents have to go elsewhere to find work or the stress drives them apart. At HHCC we strive to provide the short-term support families need to meet the basic needs of food, clothing and shelter to relieve some of that stress and help them get back on their feet."

"Okay." He came to a stop outside the door of the church day care and held up his hand. "I'm sold. Where do I send my check?"

"Oh… I…" She blushed. "I guess I do tend to sound like a fund-raiser even when I'm just answering a simple question."

"I'll bet you're good at it."

"I understand the importance of family and of how necessary the smallest things can be in making people feel that they aren't alone in facing their trials." She looked toward the gym that housed the lost-and-found area, heaved a sigh then faced Michael. "What I didn't know is if I'd find that level of need here."

"Maybe this will answer your question."

He went to the door of the day care and rapped on the glass with his knuckles. The teacher jerked her head up from the book she had been reading aloud to the cluster of kids in a semicircle around her rocking chair. She motioned for him to come in as she closed the book.

The children groaned in protest until he

walked through the door, then they all leaped up and ran for him, squealing and laughing in delight.

"It's like you're a celebrity or something." Heather laughed.

"Or something," he agreed, even as he went down on one knee to greet the littlest lambs in his flock.

Tommy Jacobs, the brown-haired, freckle-faced six-year-old whom Michael's cousin Greg Garrison had taken in as a foster child got to him first. The boy wasn't always in the day care but sometimes, when he had to, Greg left him there for an hour or so. Tommy ran up to him so fast he practically bowled Michael over.

"Have you see the signs we put up all over town looking for Charlie, Reverend Michael?" Most of the kids just called him Reverend but Tommy, used to hearing Greg and his fiancée, Maya, call Michael by his first name, often used a mix of the formal and informal. "They're everywhere. We're going to find him for sure, aren't we?"

Michael drew a deep breath, unwilling

to make such a promise. He smiled at the boy then looked up at Heather to explain, "Charlie is Tommy's dog. He's…" Michael looked at the faces of the young children. He didn't want to imply the dog was a goner, nor did he really want to remind them of the storm. "Charlie is Tommy's best friend. We're all keeping an eye out for him."

Heather smiled and nodded knowingly.

"This is Ms. Waters. She owns the cottages that some of you are staying in and she's come to High Plains…" He turned to look at her. Thoughts, emotions and memories clashed in his brain. Why *had* Heather come back? To help? She hadn't actually intended to do that herself until her worker quit. To see him? She had seemed conflicted about him and even his role as a minister. Then why? Maybe she didn't even know.

With that in mind, he decided to say aloud what he hoped for his town, for himself and not insignificantly, for the woman he had cared about for so long.

"She's come to High Plains to let us know that we aren't alone and that things are going to be all right."

Chapter Four

Michael's words stayed with Heather the rest of the day. They gnawed at her through the quick lunch they shared while Avery chatted nonstop about the town, the tornado and what she planned to do when she left High Plains at the end of the summer. The essence of his message buoyed her spirits as she made phone calls to Mary Kate to try to locate another temporary intake worker and as she let the hotel know that she'd have to cancel her reservations and would call back to make new ones as soon as she knew when she'd be leaving High Plains for Kansas City.

At the day's end, Michael's gentle reminder that "We are not alone" took on a new meaning when the families who had moved into the cottages for emergency housing welcomed her into their "homes." They all pitched in to make a potluck dinner that was finer than anything she could have imagined ordering at any of the wonderful restaurants on the Plaza. They included her in the after-dinner activities, watching the kids play volleyball and then later an almost cutthroat game of Scrabble among the adults. Not once did anyone mention the circumstances under which she had left town.

That night as she curled up on a futon in the front room of one of the cottages, Heather had wrapped herself as much in the comfort of Michael's words as she had in the patchwork quilt hastily made and cheerfully donated by a neighboring town's sewing circle.

"Knock knock." The next morning shortly before ten, Heather stood outside the open door to Michael's office in High Plains

Christian Church. She leaned her shoulder against the door frame and folded her arms over her yellow-and-white sundress. She kicked one sandal up to rest her toe against the dusty maroon carpet. "Stopped in to say good morning, let you know that you are not alone…in the building, that is, before I go downstairs to work."

He jerked his head up and said simply, "Hi."

She took a deep breath and took a moment to consider his freshly shaved face. He still had those adorable dimples, though now new lines framed his broad smile and accentuated his fabulous eyes.

"Hi." She wiggled her fingers, suddenly feeling shy around this guy she had known since she even saw him *as* a guy. Back in a time when she still thought all guys were icky. All guys but Michael… and John Parker.

"How you doing today?" he asked.

"After spending just one night in one of my family's cottages, I have to tell you, Michael, I feel really bad."

"Lumpy mattress?" A twinkle flashed in the depths of those amazing eyes.

"No." Heather pressed her hand to the small of her back. As the warmth of her palm sank into the stiff muscles, she laughed just a little. "Well, yes. But my aches will ease quickly enough. The things some of the people around here have suffered may take a very long time to set right, or get over. Some things they will never recover."

"We still haven't given up on the systematic searches." He put his hands on the desktop, which was piled high with all manner of files, books and paperwork. Given the sense of serene, even sparse order to the bookshelves behind him, she had to guess that the state of his desk had to do with the state of his congregation and their comfort with dumping things on their minister. "In fact, we have taken to gathering search parties at the drop of a hat. Or more precisely the discovery of a hat. Someone finds a few things in an area, the next thing you know everyone is out systematically searching for…whatever."

"Whatever," she murmured. "Only for most of them the 'whatever' you find lying in a field or along the road won't be enough. It won't give them the thing they really wish they could regain—a sense of security and peace of mind."

"Don't underestimate them. The searches play a part in that, too." Michael's face grew somber. He rose and came around his desk. "They remind everyone that no matter what happens the whole community is in it together. They will all pitch in with support. I do my best to help people find peace, too."

"I'm sure you do." That she never doubted. She had only to look at the man, to see him in the community at large, in the day care, with Avery and now at his piled-high desk. She knew that he was involved in every aspect of his congregants' lives. He cared.

At last she stepped fully into the room. "My misgivings are about people like me. I heard about the disaster and made an initial gift, then went on about my life."

He frowned. "You had a lot going on, Heather."

She conceded that with a nod, but could not let herself off the hook so easily. "Even so. People here were in real pain, in real need. People were hurting and I hesitated."

He crossed the last few feet between them and cupped his hand over her shoulder. "You're here now. That's what matters."

Her head heard exactly what he had said. *You're here now.* But her heart heard something else. Something more.

She looked at the man and in that instant saw the kid he had been, the minister he was now and the man he had always tried to be. A good man, one man who put High Plains first in his heart.

She stared at him and could all but hear him say what he had really meant: "You're *home* now."

She tensed. "Yeah, I guess. I am here… in town…at the church…now and ready to get to work. I should set up my intake table in the basement, right?"

"Yeah, the stage in the Fellowship Hall should give you visibility and room." He held his arm out to direct her into the hallway. "If you need anything, ask the day-care workers or just poke around until you find it. I'd love to pitch in but Avery and I were just on our way out."

"Oh?" Disappointment? Where did that come from? She shook her head and followed his direction by going into the hall. But she did not immediately head for the stairs that would take her away from him. "So you aren't sticking around today?"

"I have a meeting to tour the Old Town Hall site. After it was destroyed, the town voted to rebuild it just the way it looked in 1859."

"The Town Hall. Someone mentioned that at the cottages last night. It's a good idea to rebuild. It played such a big role around here." Funny, she'd been in town less than twenty-four hours and already she was forming an opinion on what the citizens should do. Not that she didn't have a stake in that old building, she supposed. She certainly had her share of memories there. "Remember when we used to have Little League sign-ups there every year?"

"They tried to keep the two of us from finding out about it, I'm sure."

"Hey! I wasn't a bad player." She gave him a punch in the arm just as she might have when they were nine-year-old Little League rejects. "I just…"

He grabbed her hand midpunch.

Without the impact to slow her momentum she lost her balance and she went stumbling forward half a step.

He held her as her cheek brushed his collar and he allowed her to gain her footing again. When she found her ground, he did not let go but held her gently so that her face was just inches from his.

"I just throw myself into everything I do," she whispered.

"I can see that," he said softly.

If at the moment he had leaned forward just slightly and kissed her, lightly, she would not have objected. That thought unnerved her. And made her smile.

"There you go, Heather Duster." He made sure she was steady on her feet before backing off.

"And you, Take-A-Hike Mike, just needed to learn to get out of your own way and stop waiting for everything to be perfect before you took action." As soon as the words left her mouth she realized that he might take them as a flirtatious scolding for not stealing a kiss. She flushed and hurried to clarify. "You know, when you were a kid playing softball."

"Yeah." He nodded slowly. "As a kid. Right."

"Anyway…" Heather drew the word out as she retreated in the direction of the stairwell. "I have to get going. *You* have to get going."

"We *all* have to get going." Avery came up from behind and slung her arm around Heather's shoulder as though the pair were old pals. "Let's get this Town Hall junk over with and then maybe we can do something fun. It's going to be so cool to have someone besides my uncle to talk to at stuff like this now that you're here, Heather."

"But I'm *not* here," Heather protested even as the girl pushed past her. "I mean, I'm here, in the church, but I'm not *here* in the town, not in a way that makes me part of…"

Avery had not listened to a word. She had shot out the door and down the front steps and could be heard yelling for them to hurry up from the sidewalk.

Michael gave Heather a "What can you do?" look and shrugged. "We'd love to have you come along with us to the gathering. It would be a great chance to see folks and get the word out about the work you hope your charity can do in town."

Heather took a deep breath. Despite the all the dust she inhaled, the air still smelled "churchy," like leather-bound Bibles and hymnals, and oil-soaped wood and paste and crayons from the day care and Sunday School rooms. She found great solace in the fact that some things around here had not changed.

Heather looked toward the stairwell that would lead to the basement, her work and the day care. Then she lifted her head and stared at the big gleaming wooden doors a few feet away. She did not have to peek through them to know the sanctuary waited beyond. She also found more than a little anxiety in knowing that some things here had not changed—starting with how fresh the memories still were of having her world crash in on her in that very spot. Her stomach knotted.

"Heather?" Michael jerked his thumb toward the door to urge her for an answer.

Stay and be reminded of all she had lost, of the love that the Parkers, Edward Waters and even Michael did not seem to think she deserved? Or go out to a gathering of people, put herself in the midst of the hurting and the healing and offer to do what she could to help?

No contest.

"Okay. As you said, I'm here now. Might as well make that count…while it lasts."

Chapter Five

"So, you think you'll know any of these people? Will they remember you? They all know my mom and Uncle Michael, which everyone always wants to remind me of. Then they all act like they know me but…" Avery walked as fast as she talked, as the three of them made their way down the church steps, past the preschool to the spot where the Old Town Hall had stood.

"Don't talk too long today, Reverend." Jesse Logan patted Michael on the back. "It's windy and warm enough as it is without a bunch of speech makers blowing hot air around."

"Hey, Jesse." Michael slowed and motioned for Heather and Avery to go on as he took a moment to ask, "How are you holding up?"

"The babies are coming along," he simply said, choosing instead of actually answering the question to give a report on his premature triplet daughters. Since his wife had been killed on the night of the storm, those babies had become Jesse's whole life.

Michael nodded, knowing that now was not the time to press. Let Jesse set the tone, take the lead in these matters.

"Oh, hey, and thanks for coming out and looking for my grandmother's ring. Can't imagine where it could be, but I do appreciate you and Avery spending so much time sifting through things at the ranch trying to find it." The quick change of subject told Michael he'd been right not to try to probe or get too personal.

"Anytime. If you need anything at all, just call." He gave Jesse's shoulder a squeeze and moved on toward the crowd, slowly.

He thought by not hurrying he might give Avery a chance to wear herself out a little. She would get ahead then stand in place—well, more like bounce in place—to give Heather a chance to catch up to her. Besides, hanging back allowed him to keep his distance from Heather, a chance to think and an opportunity just to look at her.

"Look at her," he murmured to himself. The sunlight gave her light brown hair a golden sheen. The yellow and white of her dress showed off the clean, healthy glow of her skin. She still walked in long strides, the way she had as a Little Leaguer determined to show the boys on the team that she could keep up with the best of them. Long strides, but nothing boyish about them, or her.

She wore well the ten years since he had last seen her. There was an ease about her, a grace that she had not had as a girl growing up in this small Kansas town.

"It will be even better than before, don't you think?" Lexi Harmon, the local vet, smiled and gave a nod of her head in the direction that Michael had been staring.

It took him a moment to realize that she meant the building, not his relationship with Heather. "Oh, yeah. I think it has…a lot of potential. At least I hope so."

He was not talking solely about the building.

Heather and Avery reached the cluster of people gathering to participate in the ground breaking for the rebuilding to begin. They stopped at the edge of the small crowd. Heather looked back at him.

He stopped in his tracks.

She smiled.

He gave her a little wave, only to find half the people in the crowd responding with waves in his direction. Suddenly, he realized that his nearly transparent crush on his old friend had him acting like a dork in front of everyone in town. And no one seemed to notice the difference from his usual behavior!

He groaned and shook his head. He was still that kid who couldn't get a hit, much less a home run—but still kept swinging! That brought to mind a verse that had played through his thoughts since Heather had agreed to stay, even if for only a while, in contrast to his own choices. His choices to stay in the game, not to act like a dork.

He laughed at himself and hustled the last few feet to join Heather and Avery and the rest of the committee and observers.

He made a point of acknowledging the other members of the group responsible for overseeing the rebuilding and getting it done in time for the Christmas Founders' Day Celebration. Glenis Appleton, along with Jesse Logan and the mayor, Gloria Lawson, all greeted him with waves or a thumbs-up to encourage him in his brief prayer for the dedication. Officer Colt Ridgeway stood off to the side. He had on his uniform, so Michael wasn't sure if he had come in an official capacity or as part of the committee. Or both.

Michael had suggested that Colt join the Rebuilding Committee. He had an inkling that it might spark something in the man who had closed himself off from life after his partner was killed and his marriage to

Lexi had ended. But Colt had not yet confirmed his commitment to the cause.

Across the way he caught a glimpse of
his cousin Greg and Greg's bride-to-be,
Maya Logan, Maya's young daughter,
Layla, and little Tommy Jacobs. They
looked good together.

He considered going over to speak to
them, but didn't, given that Greg had
already been needling Michael about his
feelings for Heather.

Better not to put Heather into that mix
until after Michael had given his prayer
and people had had a chance to share their
feelings about this special place. That's
what this day was about, after all—the
townspeople and their hope for the future.
Not Michael and his hope for…

He cleared his throat as though that
would clear his mind of all the possibili-
ties that he might have hoped for. Then his
gaze fell on Heather, who was indulging
Avery with attention and kindness. He
exhaled heavily.

The mayor, who never seemed to meet a

stranger, had worked her way through the group one handshake or hug at a time. From across the length of the cleared-away lot where the rebuilding would soon begin, she motioned to Michael. She put her hands together like a small child saying grace, held up five fingers then pointed to her wrist where she might have worn a watch.

He nodded to let her know he'd understood her message, then took a moment to collect himself. He'd been asked to say a few words about the dedication of the spot, then to give a very short and simple prayer. He had gone through materials that had all sorts of information about High Plains, but had not felt entirely satisfied. He did not want to come off as though he were reciting a list of facts or trying to give a history lesson. He had already spoken about the town, its founding and its future shortly after the storm. He didn't want to just present a short version of what he'd already done.

So he had prayed about what he would say and decided to wing it. He'd told himself that this was a good move on his part, a new boldness born of all he had gone through with his hometown this past month. In truth, he feared that Heather's arrival in town might have caused a distraction that threatened to intrude on his calling. But now as he stood among these people he loved and let his gaze find Heather in the crowd, he felt anything but distracted.

"To stand." He stood in the middle of the group a few minutes later and with those two unadorned words drew everyone's attention and quieted them down.

Avery wriggled in front of Heather and Michael grinned at his niece, then lifted his eyes and offered his old friend a subtle nod and an appreciative smile.

"Over these last few weeks, like many of you here, I have found myself turning to the Bible for comfort and answers." He ducked his head to keep the wind from blowing his hair into his eyes.

Along with keeping up with laundry, niceties like haircuts had gone by the wayside this past month. Now he regretted not letting his housekeeper trim the worst of the tumbles of brown wavy hair before she moved out of town. Still, he did not want fighting with his hair to detract from what he had to say. So he tucked his hand into the pocket of his khaki pants, raised his face and squinted just slightly into the bright August sunlight. "And time and again I have found myself drawn to Ephesians 6. I won't go into a Bible reading today, not because I don't think it applies but because it's not a whole chapter or verse that has stuck in my mind these past couple of days but just two words— *To stand.*"

He turned to make sure he included everyone as he spoke.

"We are told that if we put on the armor of God when it seems that nobody could endure the trials and hardships that besiege us, when the worst comes and seems as if it might overtake us, when all that clears away, we will still be standing."

A murmur of agreement went through the crowd.

"And we do not stand alone. We have experienced the love and support of people who have come here to do whatever they can to make our way easier. Among them Heather Waters, who immediately volunteered the Waterses' tourist cabins for housing and has now come herself to offer aid through her charity organization." He met Heather's gaze.

Spontaneous applause broke out.

Heather acknowledged it with a humble bow of her head. With her chin down, she lifted her gaze to meet his.

He took a deep breath and went on. "I know it's easy for those facing tremendous trouble, as people who have suffered so much, to think only of our own problems, of our own needs. It's natural, even, to lose sight of the fact that every day the world is filled with hurting and heartbroken people who feel they have lost everything."

He swept his gaze over the intent expressions surrounding him, letting it linger on Heather's beautiful face just a little longer than anyone else's.

"But that's not the High Plains way. This decision to restore this place that has offered so much to everyone—a place for weddings and school dances, for family gatherings and townwide events—our choice to rebuild and rededicate this special place to the town we love is proof of that."

Another murmur of agreement.

"It says that we care about things other than our own problems. It says we are here to stay." Again he sought out Heather. "It says we have seen one of those evil days that is spoken about in Ephesians and we have done, and are doing, all we can. It says that we, the citizens of High Plains, will stand."

The crowd broke into applause. Michael let it flow over him without actually taking personal pride in it. He wanted only to encourage and perhaps inspire. He wanted to capture the spirit of his fellow townspeople and honor it. He wanted to tell Heather that, no matter what had driven her away, she would always have a place here.

She met his gaze as though they were the

only two people in that open space that day. There were questions, still, in her eyes but also an intensity he had never noticed before. She studied him.

He held his hands out to his sides as if to ask, "How did I do?"

Her lips lifted on one side, but before she really broke down and gave him a full look of approval, the mayor reminded everyone that he had come to dedicate the rebuilding effort with a prayer.

Michael bowed his head and poured out words of gratitude and hope, then concluded with a quiet but forceful, "Amen."

And suddenly people swarmed around him to shake his hand, give him a hug or thank him for his insightful words. He caught a glimpse of the mayor monopolizing Heather's time and then of Avery flitting from person to person. More than once he saw the young girl pointing toward Heather and all but bursting with excitement.

That was the happiest he'd seen the kid since she'd arrived in town. All in all, he couldn't help thinking that things were turning around for Avery, as they were for High Plains and maybe even for—

"You and Heather Waters, huh?" Greg came up on Michael from behind and hooked his arm around his younger cousin's neck in a mock stranglehold. "Why didn't you tell me?"

"Tell you what?" Michael won his release with a well-placed elbow jab into his slightly larger cousin's rib cage.

"About you and—"

"That was a lovely sentiment, Michael," the mayor called out as she sent Heather off with a push as if she were launching a rowboat into High Plains River.

"And here's the lady in question," Greg said as she reached them.

"Question?" Heather turned from Greg to Michael. "Someone has questions about me?"

"Just a figure of speech," Michael rushed to assure her.

"Yeah. Like you're the lady everyone is talking about," Greg said as he stepped back to bring Heather into their conversational circle.

"People are talking about me?" The energy, confidence and grace he had noted in her earlier abruptly fell away. She bit her lower lip and cast her gaze from one man to the other.

Michael put his hand on her arm in a show of support. He wanted to make her feel at ease. He wanted her to remember that High Plains was once her home. "Nobody is talking about you, Heather."

Greg opened his mouth to say something.

"Heather, you remember my cousin Greg?" Michael took charge.

"Of course I remember Greg." Heather held out her hand, and some of the woman she had become began to rise to the surface again. "I hear congratulations are in order. Or do you offer best wishes for an engagement?"

"How'd you know about that?" Greg gave her hand a shake, but his skeptical gaze fixed entirely on Michael.

Michael gave a shrug.

"I spent the night at the cottages." Heather patted Greg's hand as she shook it, then turned to Michael and flipped her hair over her shoulder. "What did you think? That we just sat around and swapped church-lady recipes, told our favorite Bible stories?"

"That's more exciting than Mike's evenings have been in a long time," Greg teased.

"Hey!" Michael protested.

"Actually, he's a great guy, Heather. He's done a lot to hold this town together this last month."

"I'm sure he has."

"Just one aspect of the many services I am happy to provide." Michael gave a bow like a butler.

As soon as he was bent down, Greg grabbed him around the neck as though about to administer a noogie by rubbing his knuckle over his younger cousin's scalp. Instead, he leaned down close to Michael's ear and said, "You going to be ready to provide another service, say, a wedding service within the next two weeks?"

"Two weeks?" Michael pulled free from his grip and stood tall. "That soon?"

"Wedding?" Heather whispered the word.

Greg turned to her, grinning. "You should come, too. It's just a private ceremony. Doesn't seem right to have a big shindig right now with so much loss and uncertainty."

Michael opened his mouth to say something about how a wedding might help people find new hope and that, as Christians, they always had certainty in the joy of their salvation. But before he could string the words together in a way that didn't sound like an impromptu sermon, Greg slapped him hard on the back.

"But I'm sure Maya would love for you to be there, Heather, what with you practically being family and all."

"Family?" Michael almost choked on the unexpected term, not because he objected, but because he feared it would offend Heather. "You're crossing a line there, Greg, even as my cousin. It's not funny and I won't stand here and let you—"

"Me? I am not the one you need to talk to about this." He dipped his head toward a cluster of people and his gaze fixed on the figure in pink at the center.

Michael narrowed his eyes and clenched his jaw, not in anger but in frustration. "Avery!"

"I think you should know, she's telling everyone that you two are an item!"

So much for his promise that nobody was talking about Heather. Michael had to fix this—and fast.

Chapter Six

"An item?" Heather didn't know whether to crack up or crack wise, making a joke at Michael's expense. Only, she didn't find this funny.

She found it sweet and a little scary.

"You didn't believe her, did you?" she blurted out to Greg. "I mean, Michael and me? That's so…" Heather tried to laugh but it came out more like a gurgle. "We're pals. I mean, we *were* pals. Once upon a time."

"Once upon a time?" Michael frowned. "You make it sound like we stepped out of a fairy tale."

"Then I misspoke." A fairy tale? The stuff with noble knights on white horses and happy endings? She thought of herself in her wedding gown in the sanctuary and how Michael had allowed her to get to that point without saying a word. She shook her head. "We did have the kind of friendship that would have made a good story, I suppose. Until it turned into a life lesson."

"A what?" Michael put his hands on his hips and cocked his head.

"I think I'll leave you two to sort this out." Greg excused himself. "See you at the wedding, Heather? At the church. Michael will have all the info for you. He can't help but know what's going on."

Wedding. Church. Michael can't help but know what's going on. Heather tensed.

Everything in this town seemed determined to dredge up the past, to remind her that she was never wanted or good enough. That was why she'd left and why she had stayed away and why she needed to get out again and never look back.

Heather turned to head to the church.

She had a lot to do before she could leave all this behind.

"Heather, don't… I'm sorry. Avery got this crazy idea about playing matchmaker when my sister, her mom, told her…"

"You have nothing to apologize for." Heather did not look back, just held her hand up and kept walking. "This is not the worst rumor that's ever gone around this town about me. I'm sure at least this one is easily fixable because it's not true."

"*This* one? Rumors?" He caught her by the elbow and pulled her toward him. "What are you talking about?"

Feeling defensive and vulnerable, Heather tugged her arm away from Michael's restrained grasp. "If you don't know what I'm talking about then…that… I don't know."

She shaded her eyes and made a sweep of the landscape. It was so much a part of her personal history that she could close her eyes and re-create it in her mind almost down to the number of trees and bushes in the park. She focused on the spot where the old gazebo had been. But in the aftermath of the tornado that had devastated the town, it was also a place so foreign she couldn't have navigated it by starlight without getting lost.

That's how this whole trip made her feel.

"Michael, I'll be totally honest with you. If you really don't know what I'm talking about, about the rumors that people would have heard about me, then that's either really life-changing or…or it makes everything a thousand times worse."

"When you decide which it is, let me know, okay?" He moved past her briskly as though he didn't know what else to do.

She watched him go until his broad shoulders and wavy brown hair disappeared into a knot of people still mingling around their parked cars.

Did he really not know what she meant? How could that be true? The Parkers were among the wealthiest and most highly regarded families in town all those years ago. And the Garrisons were so deeply entrenched in High Plains, they had helped found the community. If any one of them knew her secret shame, then everyone did. Didn't they?

"Hey, Heather, thanks for coming to town to pitch in," someone who seemed vaguely familiar called to her from a few feet away.

She managed a smile and a nod and kept walking.

"When will you be ready to take applications for assistance?" The woman next to him, someone Heather realized she had gone to high school with, asked. "I have a family in mind to send your way."

"Um, I don't know. Maybe as soon as later today. Tomorrow for sure," she said.

"We're so glad you're here." The woman gave her a quick hug.

Heather patted the woman's back, broke free then moved on.

"Remember, if you need anything, a place to stay or volunteers, just give us a holler," came the offer from the mayor.

Everyone greeted her with open arms and, more surprisingly, open minds. She'd thought people at the tourist cottages had been nice to her because they felt beholden to her. But these people? No one seemed to hold it against her that she never knew her real father or that she had never been able to make Edward Waters love her. They did not seem to care that the Parker family had deemed her unsuitable to marry their son. None of them appeared to see her as an object of ridicule because John had left her waiting at the altar.

"If you're looking for Reverend Garrison, he headed back to the church." A blond-haired man, wearing a police officer's uniform and a hardened expression on his handsome face, came ambling toward her on the sidewalk.

"We're not an item, you know. Michael and I." She held both hands up, as though he'd caught her red-handed.

He gave the quietest chuckle she'd ever heard and muttered, "Don't believe I said you were."

"Oh, right. It's just that...we're old friends," Heather paused a moment, puzzled over how quickly that explanation had come out. "We *are* friends and will probably be working together so I just wanted that out there so nobody would get the wrong idea."

He made a show of looking in every direction. There wasn't anybody left in the street. "Consider it out."

"And if anyone asks you, Officer…?"

"Ridgeway. Colt Ridgeway." He did not offer to shake her hand but he did smile, just slightly, before his expression went somber again and he added, "I'm not generally one for gossip, ma'am."

"Yes. Oh. Right." She cleared her throat. "I have work to do."

"Me, too."

She winced out a smile and turned toward the church. So much had changed. So much had not. So many questions. So much to do. And yet she still found herself wishing there was something more she could do.

With that in mind, she looked back over her shoulder and asked, "If I wanted to organize a search for things, like that lost engagement ring, on my property by the river how would I go about doing that?"

"Not much chance of finding the ring there." He looked thoughtful, perhaps even sad for a moment before he squared his shoulders. "It's a good plan, making an organized sweep of that area now that the river has had some time to recede and things snagged along the banks have moved downstream or gotten uncovered. Why don't you check with the mayor for a day? Then you can get the word out."

"Word? You mean like in a newspaper or flyers?"

He laughed outright at that. "We have enough paper flying around here already. Just set it up with the mayor. Then let Reverend Garrison know what you decide. He'll take it from there."

"Okay. I will. Thanks." She gave him a perfunctory wave and turned to start toward the church again.

"Oh, and it wouldn't be the worst thing in the world, you know."

"What wouldn't?"

"If you and the reverend *were* an item."

Heather froze.

"He's a good man."

"I know," she whispered. "But…"

She turned in time to watch Colt Ridgeway walk away. She inhaled the hot August air and held her breath. Michael was a good man and her friend. Anything more?

She couldn't even consider it until she knew the truth about that long-ago night. Not just what he knew, but why he had done what he had done. Nothing. To do that she'd have to stay in High Plains.

Chapter Seven

"I can't do anything right." Even coming from the church kitchen a few feet down the hall, Heather could hear the whiny nuances in Avery's voice.

"This isn't about you, Avery." Michael did not take the bait.

Heather slowed down. She needed to go into the gym and to do that she had to use the door across from the church kitchen, but she did not want to intrude on Michael and Avery. Maybe if she just made a mad dash for the door she could slip in under their radar and…

"This is about me and Heather Waters."

So much for staying off the radar. She stood in the hallway and tried to decide what to do next.

"Well, there you go! That's all I was talking about at the dedication. You and Heather."

"No. There is no me and Heather."

He certainly was quick to throw that out there. She knew she shouldn't be insulted, especially as a person unintentionally eavesdropping on a private conversation. Even more so since she felt the same way—that there was nothing between her and Michael except a few shared memories. Still, hearing him be so quick to dismiss even the suggestion? It stung a little.

"Heather and I are not an item. We have never been an item. And if I'm reading all the signs correctly—"

"Everyone I told said they thought it was a terrific idea."

Silence.

Heather wished she knew what Michael was doing, how he had reacted to that news.

She pressed her palms into the fullness of the skirt of her sundress and flexed her fingers against the crisp fabric. Say something, she wanted to urge Michael.

She heard only the sounds of footsteps on the old tile floor. A cabinet opening. Dishes clattering.

She breathed in and out the dank smell of the basement and waited. She really wasn't trying to spy on Michael. She just didn't know how to proceed.

Should she march happily along as if she had heard nothing and waltz into the gym? They might not even notice her.

But that felt like a lie. A pretense at best. Michael's decision to pretend everything was just fine and dandy between her and John was at the very heart of her issues with her old friend. She had heard what she had heard. She knew what she knew.

But having just decided that nothing would make her stay in High Plains, what would be the harm in just not saying anything? Just going about her business and letting Michael deal with the girl and the fallout from whatever the girl had told people?

Heather smoothed her hands down over the places where she had unwittingly balled up the fabric of her full sundress. That was it. She'd just go about her business and in doing that get back on the road and back to her "real" life all the sooner.

"Since when have you been impressed with what people around here think is a good idea?" Michael clearly meant it as a way of teasing his niece.

Heather wished she could tell him that while that might have worked with her, a fourteen-year-old girl might see his attempt to break the tension as dismissive. As though her opinion, her wishes, her feelings were amusing, not to be seriously taken into account.

Avery did not answer her uncle.

Heather could just imagine the girl sulking. Not just any sulk, either, but a surly sulk. A surly, snarly sulk with an almost palpable glare thrown in for good measure.

She might as well have worn a sign that said "Pay attention to me," "Don't write me off," "Show that you care about me even if the only way you can show it is to punish my bratty behavior." That's what Heather would have used on Edward Waters.

And Edward would have ignored it entirely.

"Just don't do it again," Michael said, followed by the sound of a dish sliding across the countertop. "Eat your lunch and after that we can—"

Wham. Splat.

Heather jumped at the sound of a plate of food crashing to the floor.

"Avery!" Michael barked the name in surprise but with very little anger. "Why did you do that?"

"Why do I do anything? I'm a brat, remember? A loser? Nothing I do pleases you, so why shouldn't I do whatever I want anyway?"

"You are not a brat. Or a loser."

"I'm a problem child, right? You knew that before I even came here. That's *why*

my mom kicked me out and shipped me off
to this awful place to begin with."

"You are not a problem anything, Avery.
Your mom did not kick you out and I want
you to know that this place…"

Heather held her breath. What Michael
said now could make a world of difference in this young girl's life.

"I want you to know that this place is
slightly less awful because you're here."

"Oh, Uncle Michael. That's so…" The
girl's voice stretched thin. She started to
speak again but managed to strangle out a
"Nice."

Heather shut her eyes. She could hardly
swallow. Avery was trying not to cry. It got
to her. In that instant she knew how alone
and uncertain and grateful to have Michael
in her life Avery felt just then.

"I am so sorry, Uncle Michael. I didn't
mean to make trouble for you. I just
thought that you and Heather—"

"Hey, guys!" She really couldn't linger
in the hallway another moment without
making her presence known. Besides, by

walking in at the mention of her name, she made it clear that she knew they had been talking about her and she kept them from saying anything they might not have wanted her to hear.

Even if she might have liked to have heard it.

"Wow, Heather!" Michael handed Avery a paper napkin and the kid blew her nose into it as her uncle asked, "How long have you been out in the hall?"

"Long enough to know..." In only a moment of hesitation Heather did a quick mental rundown of what she had come here thinking and what she had learned in the last few minutes.

Heather wanted to get out of High Plains for good and as fast as she could.

Michael did not want even the insinuation of Heather in his personal life.

He did not have a clue what he had gotten himself into caring for a teenage girl who wished that Heather would stay and be at the very center of her uncle's personal life.

Heather understood more than anyone what the girl needed because of her own anguished childhood.

Michael was in over his head with Avery but, unlike Heather's legal father, Michael wanted to see eye-to-eye with the kid, to love her and help her find her way in life.

Except he didn't have a clue…

That brought them full circle. Heather knew what to do.… Michael and Heather had no desire to spend any more time together…

But Avery needed them both.

Heather looked at the food on the floor and the kid wiping tears from her reddened eyes with a stiff paper napkin.

"I was out in the hall long enough to know that there is a lot of work to be done around here and if I plan to be of service to the folks of High Plains, I am going to need an assistant." She stepped forward and extended her hand to the young girl, knowing that if the kid and Michael agreed she would be giving up the rest of her free time and maybe more to honor her commitment. "What do you say, Avery? Would you like to help me set up a special project to, um, let's say, make High Plains a lot less awful?"

Chapter Eight

"How'd you know?" Michael asked Heather as he lugged a heavy box for her through the doors of the gym and the Fellowship Hall later that afternoon.

A few of the members of his congregation had come over to help set up tables and organize the stacks of paperwork required to apply for aid from Heather's organization. As they hustled around, hunting down chairs and pencils and clipboards, Avery sat in the plush chair from his office at the large table at the center of the stage, working away on Heather's sleek, powerful laptop.

He plunked the box in his arms down and pushed his fingers back through his hair to keep the sweat-dampened curls from clinging to his forehead. "How did you know that putting Avery in charge of this Web site idea of yours would totally refocus and reenergize her?"

His niece's fingers clicked and clattered over the keyboard so rapidly that it was hard to believe she wasn't just striking random keys. But the sound of chimes signaling incoming mail and the sudden joy of an "aha" moment breaking over the girl's fresh face told him she was accomplishing a lot.

"You assign her this task, give her a title, turn her loose and just like that—" he snapped his fingers "—she's like a new kid."

"It's not rocket science." Heather folded her arms and paused, shifting her gaze to catch his.

When his eyes met hers, his breath caught for only a moment before it dawned on him that she'd made a joke. He laughed, but not because he found it funny. In truth, he wasn't even sure what she had said. He laughed because it felt so good to have her here. To know that she felt relaxed enough at last to tease him the way they had as kids. To discover, even in the depths of loss and chaos, that God still moved through the loving hearts of His children.

Michael wanted Heather to stay in High Plains. If not forever then long enough to give him the chance that he had never had since that summer when she and John fell in love. He wanted her to stick around long enough to find out if she could love him.

"You're saying that this clash of personalities with Avery just needed a woman's touch?" he asked.

"No. Though, I guess…" She looked toward the girl throwing herself into the task at hand, working with Heather's assistant in Wichita to set up a special Web page to collect donations for High Plains. "Just someone who could empathize with a kid who just wanted to be loved."

He studied her for moment, long enough to know that he did not dare say what was really on his mind, in his heart. *I love you, Heather. I always have.*

Instead, he stuck with the more general, and decidedly more ministerly, "All of us just want to be loved, Heather."

"Yes, but not everyone finds love, Michael." Her shoulders sank. She angled her head down slightly, though her eyes stayed fixed on the activity on the stage.

She looked so lost. So alone. So much like she had as a kid, like she had on the day John Parker had broken her heart.

"Some of us only seem to find lies and rejection," she murmured.

"Then maybe those people are looking in the wrong places," he murmured.

Look at me. He tried to will her to raise her world-weary gaze to his. To see him and the heart he was ready to lay open before her.

"I know you love Avery. I hope you don't think I meant otherwise." She pulled her shoulders up and turned to him. "And I know your sister does, too. You are all acting in her best interest. She might not see it now, but she will."

Michael exhaled in a huff, concern twisting the muscles in his back and neck into a knot. "I hope you're right."

"I know I am." She angled her chin up, then pointed to the cumbersome box at his feet and crooked her finger to remind him that he still had a ways to go. As she led him toward the stage, she kept talking. "When people have their feelings hurt, feel alienated and tempted to fall into self-pity, the best way to get them to, as you say, look in the right places, is to get them to look beyond themselves."

Michael hoisted the burdensome box high against his chest and followed, secretly wishing she would at least glance back to see what light work he found the job. Not usually a vain guy, just this once he longed for her to notice the changes this past month of hard work had brought about. Chopping tree branches, moving brush, hauling away rubbish, even helping people patch roofs and mend fences—and in the literal sense, not just the kind of fence mending he usually did as a small-town minister—might not have made him less of a klutz but it did make him stronger, more buff than usual.

"Get people involved in something bigger than themselves. Especially young people who naturally tend to think the world revolves around them." She walked onto the steps that went to the back of the stage, oblivious to his bulging biceps. "It lends a sense of perspective that adds depth and meaning. Purpose brings its own kind of fulfillment."

"Is that what you did?" So Heather hadn't seen this new physical aspect to him. She had done something better. She'd just revealed a little bit of herself, of not just who she had become since they'd parted ways but how and why. "Is that how you came to take on a whole charity organization and the issues of hundreds of hurting families?"

Heather froze.

Clearly he had touched on a sensitive spot. If she had been just another social worker come to town as part of her job, he'd have let it go. But this was Heather. His friend. The woman he had loved and who, to this day, held something against him that she would not share. He had grown physically stronger by facing resistance head-on—tree limbs, rubbish, roofs, fences. He wanted to know now if she had done the same thing. Had she found that overcoming the things that weighed her down, blocked her way, hemmed her in had made her stronger? Or had she simply maneuvered around them?

"And did it work for you, Heather? Does the life you lead now have new meaning? Have you found fulfillment away from High Plains? Or are you still looking for the love your father and John Parker denied you?"

Heather whirled around, her eyes flashing fury. "How dare you talk to me about John and love and my father! After you…you…"

Michael staggered backward but kept his balance. "I what, Heather? You keep alluding to this thing that I've done, that you still hold against me but—"

"Talk about your past coming back to

haunt you!" At that moment the mayor, Gloria Lawson, came wheeling a dolly piled high with heavy, oversize books from the opposite side of the stage. The metal supports hit the wooden floorboards. The force of a sudden stop sent books spilling and sprawling in every direction.

Gloria laughed in delight, then bent to retrieve the nearest one, which she held up high for all to see. "I bring for your enjoyment and chagrin every yearbook, Chamber of Commerce publication, church scrapbook and newspaper clipping kept by local civic and social clubs that I could find among the town employees. I think someone even dug up a phone book from 1976!"

"Cool!" Avery shot up out of her chair. "We've got the bugs knocked out of the Web site and Heather's assistant, I mean Heather's *other* assistant, Mary Kate, is drafting the official e-mail now. When she's done, we can send it out to potential donors and people wanting to lend support in whatever way they can."

The young girl hurried to the jumble of

books and papers that the mayor had delivered and dove in. She only looked up long enough to nail Michael with a warning look. "Are you going to help, Uncle Michael?"

"I was, uh…" He held the box up; the weight of it shifted and he had to brace himself against the wall to keep from dropping it.

He met Heather's gaze and considered announcing that he and Heather were in the middle of something important.

Before he could speak for both of them, Heather tipped up her nose and said, "I have to talk to the mayor."

He watched Heather join Avery and the mayor in cleaning up the mess before he brought the box over to them and said, "I brought up some more things to possibly cull names and addresses from."

"Isn't this wonderful, everyone pitching in like this, giving people who care about our little town specific and meaningful ways to contribute, as well?" the mayor asked as she paused to stare at the black-and-white photos in an old yearbook for a moment. "I can't thank you enough for this, Heather. You always were the bright one. Wasn't she, Michael?"

"She always brightened my days." He sat the box down and stole a look at the woman in the yellow sundress.

She gave him a look that was anything but sunny.

"Heather, you are just what we needed around this place. A new pair of eyes bringing a new perspective. I tell you, your coming home has been good for High Plains, and I expect only more good things to come of it."

"I haven't come—" Heather called out, but the mayor was already deep in a rapid-fire conversation with the equally excited Avery. "Home," she concluded just above a murmur.

She hadn't come home. He had to remember that. She had not come to stay. He wanted her to, but more than that he wanted her to be happy. He had always wanted, above all, for her to be happy.

He had not understood when they were

younger that other people, even people you think you love enough to share your life with, cannot make you happy. Faith, hope, work and inner peace—if a person didn't have those, then happiness would remain elusive.

In order to have those and savor them fully, Heather would, at some point, have to confront her deepest fears and address the old hurts. Until she did that, she would never really feel at home anywhere.

"Actually, Mayor, I wanted to talk to you about organizing a search around the cottages," Heather called out to the sixty-something woman bustling around to organize the books and material she had just brought in.

"Oh, that's a great idea, Heather. You really have come at a good time. I can't tell you how much we're all looking forward to having you as part of our community again."

Heather opened her mouth, probably to offer a protest, but nothing more than a squeak came out as she stood there, center stage, with her hands limply at her sides.

Michael couldn't help himself. He

wanted her to be happy and that meant he couldn't leave this alone.

"Funny thing about getting involved in something bigger than yourself. Sometimes it creates a giant smokescreen for us to hide behind. But other times?"

She jerked her chin up slightly and looked at him from the corners of her eyes.

"Other times it demands so much of us that we have no choice but to grow big enough ourselves to be equal to the opportunities and challenges it gives us."

Chapter Nine

Heather mulled that over the rest of the day and through that night—as she helped get the workstation in order, as she helped Avery set up the outreach program to solicit donations to help the families of High Plains, even as she consulted the occupants of the cottages about a good day to do the search. Michael's caution stayed with her.

"By getting involved in something bigger than yourself, you may have to grow in order to meet the challenges and opportunities it offers." She repeated the gist of it over the slap of her shoes on the church basement floor the next morning.

She had often found that true in her work, but in her personal life?

Heather scrolled down through the voice messages on her cell phone and sighed.

Who was she kidding? Heather didn't *have* a personal life.

And did it work for you, Heather? Does the life you lead now have new meaning? Have you found fulfillment away from High Plains? Or are you still looking for the love your father and John Parker denied you? Again, Michael's words invaded her thoughts.

She just couldn't seem to get away from the man.

She looked around at the church where she had spent so much of her youth, the church that her one-time friend and teammate now pastored. Maybe she shouldn't *want* to get away from Michael Garrison.

Maybe, just maybe, he was part of a "something bigger" that would finally help her resolve her past and grow beyond the old hurt and disappointment. Except that Heather couldn't help remembering that Michael's behavior was inextricably entwined with those old hurts and disappointments.

John Parker had had something at stake when he turned his back on Heather that day. He was looking at taking a step he clearly was not ready to make, taking a vow for a lifetime commitment that would not have lasted more than a few years. In many ways John Parker had done her a favor, and she could understand his reasons. Still, it hurt that not only had he *not* loved her, but he had also cared so little about her that he hadn't broken off their engagement in person.

But Michael. He had withheld the truth and let her be publically humiliated, left at the altar. She supposed he thought she deserved it.

"No," she murmured to herself. As furious as the memory made her, even now, she could not believe that of him. All these years she had focused on *what* Michael had done and never on *why*. That was the answer she needed now.

"I still can't find it." Avery, dressed in

baggy denim shorts rolled up to her knees and a faded baseball T-shirt for a team sponsored by Mama's Pizzeria, sat on the floor of the stage. Stacks of old yearbooks and phone books and newspapers circled her.

Heather climbed the steps to the stage and placed her laptop, phone and the files of applications that already needed reviewing onto the table and squinted thoughtfully at the girl. "Find what?"

Avery looked up, her thick brown hair pulled into a bouncy ponytail and a hint of mischief in her face. "A yearbook with you and Uncle Michael in it."

Heather tucked her phone into the pocket of her too-chic-for-the-circumstances wraparound dress and frowned. "I thought there was one from our freshman year."

"Yeah, but you had a block that said 'Photo not available' and someone drew a mustache on Uncle Michael in that one."

"That would have been me." Heather put her hand over her face and winced, though she couldn't help but laugh. "I know exactly whose yearbook you've gotten hold of, too. She had a crush on your uncle that year so I, most considerately, did her the favor of showing her how he'd look when he grew up."

Avery grabbed the book, peered at it then held it up for Heather to see, as well. "Not even close!"

Heather studied the sweet young face of the man who had been on her mind so much of late. Good face. Good guy. Good thing he never grew a mustache. She smiled and shook her head. "I thought I was doing the girl a favor."

"I think you were doing yourself a favor." Avery hopped up and came to the intake table, laying the book down as she did.

"How?" Heather brushed her fingertips over the cover of the old book.

"By trying to scare that girl off so you could keep Uncle Michael all to yourself."

"Me and Michael?" Heather choked out a chuckle then shook her head, flipped open her laptop and turned it on, staring at the screen as it came to life, as though the world depended on her concentrating on what happened next. "I don't *think* so."

"Maybe that's the problem—you think too much. Maybe sometimes you should just go with it."

"Me? I hardly think at all!" That didn't come out the way she meant it. "It's your uncle who overthinks things."

"Okay, prove it." Avery reached out, snagged Heather by the wrist then gave a firm tug. "Come with me."

"Come with you where?"

Avery turned as she spoke and actually began to walk away as she said, "To the Parish House to find Uncle Michael's yearbooks."

"The…?" Heather tugged back and when that didn't win her release, she dug in her heels. Or did the best she could, since she was actually wearing heels—small ones—and standing on a polished wooden stage floor. "Oh, no! We can't just barge into your uncle's home first thing in the morning like this."

"It's *my* home, too, at least for now." Avery

stopped pulling on Heather's arm, but she did not let go of her wrist. "I'm asking you to come to my house, Heather. Please?"

If any other kid in the world had asked her, Heather could have played the professional social worker card and handled this with a flat refusal. But this girl?

Heather had known Avery as a toddler, babysat her with Michael. This girl felt like something of an outcast in High Plains and an oddball in her own family. This girl tried her best to never let anyone see her cry, even though she probably felt like crying every day. How could she refuse her?

Heather slid her fingers along the top of her laptop and exhaled slowly. "Give me a minute to—"

"Don't think it to death, just do it."

Heather considered injecting a life lesson here. Hadn't the girl come to High Plains to help curb her impulsiveness, which led to bad choices? Then again, she had also been sent here to make better connections, to learn to respect and engage with others. That's exactly what she was doing right now. "Okay, but at least let me go wash my hands and face first."

"Are you kidding? You look awesome."

"Oh, thanks." Heather ran her hand under the upturned collar of her dress and ducked her head. "I packed for a couple of weeks' shopping and relaxing in Kansas City. I don't really have work clothes and, of course, there's nowhere here to get any."

"There's a clothes closet of things people donated. I'm sure they won't mind if you borrow a few things. Uncle Michael has been doing that off and on when he can't get his laundry done."

"Oh, so that explains it. I thought, the way he's been dressed these past few days, that he just had dreadful taste in clothes," Heather joked as she followed the girl off the stage.

"Oh, he *does*." Avery glanced back and grinned. "He's just applying his lack of fashion sense to a wider selection of stuff now.

"Uncle Michael? I'm back and I brought company!" Avery practically blasted through the front door of the Parish House.

Heather lingered in the open doorway, hesitant to cross the threshold. She had visited the quaint old bungalow-style home many times as a kid. She couldn't look anywhere without stirring a memory of a Youth Group meeting, a counseling session or a holiday open house. She looked toward the corner where a huge Christmas tree would have stood. Then to the dining room table that had practically groaned from the weight of an Easter Sunday buffet. Then her gaze fell on the double doors that led to the pastor's study.

Though they were closed, Heather knew exactly what lay beyond those heavy, almost foreboding doors. She had all but memorized every detail when she and John had gone there to go over their wedding plans.

She hugged her arms tightly around herself, but that did not keep the chill from wrapping its icy fingers around her heart. She shouldn't have come here.

"Hey, Heather, no thinking too much about everything, remember?" Avery waved to motion her inside.

"I…uh… Maybe I shouldn't have come." She held back. "There's so much work to do back at the church. I don't feel right wasting too much time on personal matters."

"Oh, stop it. Really! Uncle Mike's in the kitchen. Go grab some coffee or something. Feeding yourself isn't wasting time on personal stuff, is it?" Avery rushed by in a blur. "He says his old yearbook is in the basement. I'll bring it in here when I find it."

Heather considered arguing that she should have coffee at the workstation in the church, but just *who* would she make that case to? Avery had disappeared through a doorway, her footsteps as subtle as a charging herd of elephants on the creaking old basement staircase.

"Michael?" Finally she came fully inside the house. It looked the same as it had ten years ago. Proof, she decided, of Avery's thoughts on Michael's lack of interest in things like fashion and home decor. It spoke to Heather, who held dear her own ideas about living simply in order to serve others, of Michael's dedication to his work and his congregation and…

Oh, who was she kidding? The fact that the place looked virtually untouched since its previous owner all but screamed— "Michael Garrison does not now nor has he in the last five years had a girlfriend he was serious enough about to let her try to make this place more homey!"

Heather supposed that as a good friend that could have made her quite melancholy.

But it didn't.

She smiled to herself and headed toward the kitchen at the back of the house. Of course she didn't wish for Michael to be alone or without love in the world, but knowing he didn't have anyone serious in his life gave Heather a reason to wonder: Was there room in Michael's life for a significant other? And, if so, was there even a chance that she might like to be the one?

The *one?*

She held her breath and asked herself where that thought had come from.

Heather Duster and Take-A-Hike Mike? Not likely.

The jilted bride and the disapproving best man? Never!

But the minister and the social worker? The woman life had helped to make her and the man Mike had become?

A muffled jangle of the phone carried through the closed kitchen door, startling Heather.

"Garrison," Michael answered abruptly, so abruptly that Heather could hear that he hadn't quite finished his mouthful of food.

She rubbed her temple and looked down at the adorable shoes she had bought just for her trip—marked down, of course, and traditional enough that she'd be able to wear them for years to come.

"The preacher with, let's see…" She spoke under her breath and ticked Michael's attributes off on her fingers as she listed them. "No fashion sense. Who waits to act until he thinks he can please everyone. But who never hesitated to answer his calling."

She wriggled the three fingers she had held up then switched hands to counter with her own list. "And the social worker with the guilt complex that never allowed her to even buy a pair of shoes unless she could justify them as practical. Who is afraid she will never be lovable. Who throws herself into her work but maybe isn't exactly sure why."

She wanted to laugh, but it really did sort of have its own beautiful logic, didn't it?

And what was holding her back from exploring the possibility? She looked at the doors to the study where she and John had prepared for a marriage that never came to be.

"Why didn't you just tell me, Michael? Why didn't you trust me with the truth, as miserable as it was?" She looked to the kitchen door again.

She had changed so much over the past ten years. Was it really so hard to believe that Mike had, as well?

She knew one way to find out.

She took a deep breath, threw back her

shoulders and marched into the kitchen. "I heard something about coffee being served—"

Michael held one finger up to ask her to hold her thought. With his other hand he pressed his phone to his ear and listened intently. "Uh-huh."

"Should I?" She pointed to the still-swinging kitchen door.

He shook his head. "Hold on, sis." He held the phone away from his mouth. "It's my sister. There's been, let's call it a development, in the Avery saga."

Heather turned away. It felt like a betrayal, or at least presumptuous, for her to be in on any news concerning Avery, even before the girl herself knew what was going on. "It's no problem for me to just wait out—"

"When is the court date?" Michael asked into the phone again.

"Court date?" Heather froze with her hand to the door. She glanced back over her shoulder.

"Oh, right. Right. Of course." Michael motioned for her to come into the kitchen.

He even pointed to the coffeemaker and cups on the counter, then at the chair across from his. Even as he welcomed Heather into his kitchen, he asked his sister on the other end of the line, "So what do you want to do about Avery?"

"I really think I should give you—" and by *you* she actually meant Avery "—some privacy."

The old brass hinges squeaked as she gave the door a push outward.

"Stay." He held his hand up and gave her a look. He was tired and worried and yet so strong in his faith, in his role in his family that he made Heather feel solid and safe, just looking at him. "Please?"

He was a good man. A real man. Not the callow kid he had once been. Heather smiled, slipped into the chair across from him and sighed.

Michael's lips twitched up on one side. Not quite a smile, but it sent a warm glow through her just the same.

"Yes. I agree," he told his sister on the phone. "Do you want to talk to her?"

Heather put her hands on the edge of the table, ready to spring up and go fetch the girl from the basement.

He shook his head to stop Heather from taking action, then ran his hand back through his hair as he exhaled slowly, then told his sister, "Okay, leave it to me, then."

Heather's shoulders relaxed against the back of the old wooden kitchen chair.

"Yeah. Right. I get it. I know. Yes. I love you, too. I will. I'll use my best judgment. Bye." Michael clicked the button to end the call.

He stared at the silent black handset for a moment. Then he set it aside. Without meeting Heather's gaze, he folded his arms on the table, laid his head down and groaned.

She longed to reach out and stroke his head, to feel those coarse curls coil around and through her fingers. She wished she knew how to make it all better for him.

In a flash she wondered if that's how he had felt that day in the church. Had he seen her pain and confusion and wished he could do something, anything to make her feel better?

Until she had come back to High Plains, she'd have curtly and unflinchingly answered that with a resounding "no." But now she wondered if maybe he had just been too young and inexperienced to know that all he would have had to do was reach out to her and ask, "You want to tell me about it?"

"I don't want to tell *anyone* about it," he muttered into his arms.

Her stomach clenched into a cold knot. He was shutting her out. Not trusting her with the truth. She looked at the top of his head and her fingers flexed. Maybe instead of caressing his head she should stretch out, grab him by his thick, wavy hair and bang his thick, stubborn head against the table until she knocked some sense into him.

She rolled her eyes and nudged his knee with her toe under the table instead. "You felt pretty free giving me some advice earlier, pal. Let me share a little with you now."

"Huh?" He shifted his head so that only

his compelling blue eyes and the bridge of his nose showed over his folded arms.

She lowered her own head until her chin almost touched the red-and-white gingham place mat on the old oak table. When their gazes locked, she spoke quietly but distinctly to remind him, "Some things cannot be put off until *you* are ready to deal with them."

"You think I don't know that?" He raised his head fully.

She did the same and laced her arms over her chest to add a bit of attitude. "Did you or did you not get pretty cocky chiding me about getting involved in my work and things bigger than myself, suggesting that I might not have always thought through what it would demand of me?"

"I, uh, I *think* that was me." Just the slightest hint of a grin played over his lips.

"Well, there was another side to that coin." She wagged her finger at him, to drive home both that she meant business and that she wasn't so much angry as determined to make her point. "Doing things in God's time doesn't always mean waiting."

"I think I see the yearbooks—be up in a sec." Avery's voice carried faintly up from the basement.

Michael looked toward the door, then at the phone he had just gotten the clearly troubling news over. At last he looked at Heather. "You think so, huh?"

"I do." She held her hand out to him across the table, palm up. "Sometimes, Take-A-Hike Mike, God's time is now."

Chapter Ten

Michael hesitated only a moment before he took Heather's hand and gave it a squeeze. "It wasn't that I wanted to shut you out, Heather. I just...well, you're in town for such a short time and the situation with Avery is a total mess and I don't know how...or when...it's going to really work out."

There, that wasn't so hard, she wanted to tell him. She didn't need to know everything, she just needed for him to be up-front with her. If only he had been that candid with her ten years ago, then... *Then what?*

"You don't have to tell me anything." She inhaled the aroma of coffee and it reminded her that she had work to get to. "I know you'll figure it out and do the right thing."

"Really?" Michael pushed the nearly antique chair back from the table so forcefully that it squawked and creaked. He picked up his plate in one hand and his coffee mug in the other. The thin, blue, fluted paper with muffin crumbs still clinging to it fell to the floor. "You think I can get a handle on the disenfranchised, angry teenager thing and actually do some good for Avery?"

"Absolutely," she said. "Just keep in mind that Avery is a great kid. She is bright and capable of understanding and dealing with the truth if you give her the chance."

He stood. "It means a lot to me to hear you say that, Heather."

"Good." She bent, swept up the fallen paper muffin cup and stood just as he stepped forward to take his plate and mug to the sink.

"Yeah," he murmured, standing just inches from her.

For a second she just stood there, so close

she could see every detail of his face. His eyelids drooped slightly, casting the usually playful glint in his eyes in shadow that only intensified his probing gaze. His pale lips did not curve upward at the corners and yet, from this vantage point she could still see the outline of his dimples.

"You…" She raised her hand and brushed her fingers over his cheek lightly.

His eyes grew wide at her touch.

"Muffin crumb," she explained.

"Oh." He chuckled. "I can shepherd a flock, head emergency operations for the entire town and, according to you, cope with teenage angst, but I still don't seem to have the whole feeding-myself-without-making-a-mess thing mastered."

She nodded. Unsure of what to say, unsure of what to feel.

This, the two of them alone in the small kitchen of Michael's home with the morning sunlight streaming in, was the closest Heather had ever been to actually feeling like she belonged. Like she had a home.

Or that she *could* have a home. Maybe

someday, in time, if she and Michael could find their friendship again and build on that. If she could be sure he did not harbor the same opinion of her that the Parker family had, that her own father had. That she was unworthy.

If only she knew that he did not hold her history against her. If she only believed without a doubt that he had changed and would never withhold information, as he had in the past.

"Michael?" She tipped her head.

"I'm glad you're back in High Plains, Heather." He tipped his head, too, mirroring her pose. "I hope you stay a while."

Maybe she didn't have to ask him outright what he thought of her. Words, like tears, didn't change things. Actions did. Maybe it was time she started paying attention to Michael's actions and let those tell her what she needed to know. "Thank you, Michael."

"Found it!" Avery shouted from the basement in triumph. "Just have to move these…"

There was a loud crash, then, "Nothing's busted!"

Nothing in the basement may have broken, but Avery's intrusion broke the brief, intense connection between Heather and Michael.

Heather moved around him to throw the paper muffin cup in the trash can in the corner of the kitchen.

Michael's plate and mug clattered against the bottom of the deep enamel sink.

"Speaking of staying a while," he said as he turned and rubbed his hand along the back of his neck. "I guess that's what Avery will be doing."

"What?" She went to the sink and flipped on the water to wash her hands. "Why?"

Michael moved to the swinging door and peeked out of it. After a moment, he let it fall shut and focused his attention on Heather. "One of the friends my sister thought was such a bad influence on Avery was just picked up on charges of shoplifting."

"Not good."

"Gets worse."

Not seeing a dish towel, Heather settled for just shaking her hands dry.

"She was shoplifting cigarettes and had been drinking."

"Oh, no." A shower of tiny droplets of water went flinging onto her arms and dotting her bright green dress. Combined with the August heat and the heightened emotion in the room, the sudden sensation made her shiver. "And your sister is worried that Avery might have been doing the same thing? If it helps, I haven't seen any evidence of that."

He nodded then looked out the door again.

There were sounds of Avery struggling to take care of whatever had fallen over in the basement. The teenager grunted and groaned and finally must have kicked something. A thump. A thud. A curse word.

"Yeah. We haven't seen it here, but she's been pretty isolated. If she were back in that environment again, who knows what would happen?"

Heather leaned back against the counter

and crossed her arms. "You can't judge people by the company they keep, Michael."

"Maybe not, but my sister also wants to do everything she can to keep Avery in better company."

Heather didn't want to take that personally. After all, she was the person Michael allowed to spend the most time with his niece. And yet, the unloved and harshly judged teen that Heather had once been, the girl she had never completely left behind, couldn't help hearing a tinge of accusation in his words. You are judged by the company you keep. John Parker and Edward Waters had decided that Heather was bad company.

"What does that mean, you want to keep her in better company?" Heather wanted to know.

"It means exactly that for now. My sister wants Avery to remain in High Plains."

Heather relaxed. "That's not too bad."

"If this were June or July, maybe." He let the door fall shut and moved behind one of the chairs. He braced his arms straight against it. His features seemed to close, giving him a pained, pinched expression. "But because it's August, if Avery stays now it means that in roughly ten days she'll have to start school. And if she starts school in High Plains, she'll need to stay here through at least the end of the fall semester."

"How do you think she'll react to that news?" Heather asked, hoping to get Michael to think about Avery and how he should deal with the issue.

"I guess…" Michael exhaled and shook his head. He looked down at the table and ran both hands back through his hair. "I don't… She won't like it but—"

"Everything's cool, y'all! I took care of the stuff in the basement and found this!" Avery came bursting through the door holding up the high school yearbook from Michael and Heather's senior year. "You two were pretty cute in high school!"

"I think some of us are pretty cute now," Michael shot back as he adjusted his shoulders in his borrowed blue-and-yellow bowling shirt.

Avery nailed Heather with an unbelieving look and held it for a moment before they both broke into peels of laughter at Michael's expense.

The guy ate it up.

He did a little turn like a model on a catwalk, ran his hands through his hair to make it stand up the way it was in the photo, then struck the same pose—head turned, chin down—as his senior portrait.

More laughter.

"Your turn," Avery said, flipping the pages until she reached the last row of photos. She stabbed her finger down on a photo of Heather, perfectly dressed in the latest and most expensive clothes that her father could provide. "There you are."

Her hair had not changed much since then. She wasn't heavier, nor did she really have many more signs of age. But when Heather stared at the two-dimensional image from another time, she felt she was looking at a total stranger. Edward Waters's daughter, or so she thought. A girl who thought she'd marry and make a home in High Plains and never leave. That was the girl who loved John Parker and trusted that Michael Garrison would always be her best friend.

"There I am," Heather murmured as she traced her fingertip over the innocent face staring up at her from the page.

She had grown so much.

Michael had, as well.

"You two sure were a couple of cuties." The glossy pages rippled as Avery flipped back to Michael's photo then back to Heather's then back again. "Why didn't you ever get together? You know, romantically?"

"Because of…" Michael stopped the girl's ruffling through the yearbook, flipped a page then jabbed his finger down firmly. "Because of him."

"Wow. Supercute guy." She jerked her head up to grin at Heather. "Your boyfriend?"

"Fiancé." Michael muttered the correction then cleared his throat and said loud and clearly, "And my best friend since we were kids."

"My best friend, too." Heather felt compelled to remind Michael of that before turning toward Avery and adding, "We were all the best of friends since we were eight or nine, I think. They called us the Three Amigos."

"Really?" Avery practically pounced on Heather. "What happened? Why did you pick him instead of Uncle Michael? Was there a love triangle like in the movies? Why didn't you marry this guy?"

"Avery!" Michael frowned.

"I'm just curious. This is the first I've heard of any of this. I mean, Mom told me about the girl and I'm not stupid, I know Heather *is* the girl but—"

"Avery, enough!" he cautioned her though gritted teeth.

"The girl?" Heather homed in on the term Avery had used before. "What is she talking about, Michael?"

He clenched his jaw tighter for a moment, then blew his breath out in a long blast of resignation. "Okay. I guess there's no harm in telling you. I mean, I can't believe you don't already know this but…when we were kids, up to and including the time you and John got together…I had…sort of…a…little bit of…a…crush on you."

"You did?" Heather had had no idea. She must have been so caught up in her feelings for John and her hope for finally having a real home.

No excuse, she thought. All these years she had held Michael's action, or lack of action, against him. Yet she had never stopped to consider that there might be other things at play besides her own pain. She expected him to have taken her feelings into account, but had never given him the same courtesy. "I can't believe I never knew that. A crush? On *me?*"

Michael lowered his head. His shoulders rose and fell in an amused "no big deal" gesture. When he lifted his gaze to hers, though, she could tell that it *was* a big deal, not something he had divulged lightly. "It was a long time ago."

Heather pressed her lips together, not sure how to answer that. So many memories ran through her mind, so many questions.

"What about now?" Avery asked, beating them both to the punch.

Heather turned to face Michael, only to find the young teen staring right at her. "Me? You're asking *me* what about now?"

"Uncle Michael won't be the first one to say anything." Avery took the yearbook from him and held it out so that Heather could see the photo of John Parker. "So you were friends then and friends now and Uncle Michael wanted to be more than friends then and you're both here now and you didn't marry this guy. So I don't think it's such a big shocker that I'd ask, what about now?"

Heather held her breath. She looked at the photo of the young man, taken ten years ago—the man she had thought she would spend the rest of her life with. She felt absolutely nothing.

"So?" Avery prodded again. "Any shot of you two getting together now?"

Heather raised her gaze to Michael. She bit her lower lip. She folded her arms to keep her hands from trembling. Her stomach took a tumble.

"Now?" She exhaled and smiled at the man, slowly. "Now we're both a part of something bigger than ourselves. That's the priority. We have work to do, but who knows what there will be time for when the dust settles?"

Chapter Eleven

Who knows what there will be time for when the dust settles?

Michael didn't think he'd ever invested so much hope in such a nonanswer in his whole life.

He arrived at the river cottage cleanup and search site well after work had begun. It was a terrific day for it—hot and sunny but not overpoweringly so, as was often the case in August. They had waited long enough after the last big rainfall for the waters to recede. Perfect conditions for working on the cottages and combing the riverbanks for remnants of the storm.

"Hey, Uncle Michael! 'Bout time you showed up! Look what I found already." Avery reached into the armload of things she had recovered and raised a picture frame with broken glass. "You better get busy."

"She's been hustling all morning." Heather came up behind him, tugging off her heavy cotton work gloves as she did. "She has a servant's heart, Michael."

He looked at the progress around the cottages since Heather had arrived just a week earlier. The small one- and two-bedroom cottages could use a coat of their traditional gray paint, but the grounds around them looked neat. With the trim and roofs all freshly patched, a couple of them sported brand-new doors and all of them had storm windows in place, something he hadn't seen on the places left neglected by Heather's father for years.

Then he looked at Heather. With her hair caught up in a knot, she already had the pink tinge of a sunburn starting on her exposed neck. The clothes she'd borrowed from the clothes closet at the church were already grubby from work and her un-adorned face—and more gorgeous for the lack of makeup and effort—shone with the glow of having worked up a good sweat.

"Avery has a servant's heart?" He grabbed her hand and flipped it over to check out the beginning of a blister on her index finger. "Takes one to know one."

She slid her hand free and gave the beat-up old work shirt he had thrown on—his own for a change—a tug. "I was going to say it must run in the family."

"I'm sorry I didn't get here sooner. Had some minister business to take care of."

"Everyone understands. They all made a point of telling me how you and Avery really put in a lot of hours already doing this kind of thing, searching places like the church and the Circle L Ranch, not to mention running the lost and found."

"Yeah. We really had hoped to find the Logan family's heirloom ring out at the ranch. I can't figure out how so many things have been uncovered and yet that ring still hasn't turned up."

"It will, eventually. At least I hope so." She transferred her work gloves from her right hand to her left. "I know it symbolizes a lot."

"Yeah." Michael nodded. "Speaking of engagement rings, that's what kept me this morning. Greg and Maya are finalizing their wedding plans. Seems his father will be able to attend, so that's really good news."

"I'm happy for them."

She didn't look happy. She looked…like a woman recalling her own engagement lost and the relationship with her father never mended.

"Heather…"

"So… You're late but with an admirable excuse." She slapped her gloves together. "Don't think that's going to make me go easy on you. There's still plenty of work to do around here. Plenty of land along the river to go over with a fine-tooth comb."

She started off toward the river and an unoccupied stretch of high weeds and brush.

"I don't think I brought a fine-tooth comb," he said as he hurried after her.

She gave him a beady-eyed glare over her shoulder, then shook her head. "Doesn't surprise me a bit, since it looks like you styled your hair by sticking your head in a blender today."

He paused to rub his hand through the waves, trying in vain to smooth it down a bit. "Yeah. I haven't exactly had time to get to the barber this last month."

"If you'd like, I could trim it for you." She marched on toward the river, calling out loudly behind her as she did, "It won't be high style, but then…"

"Neither am I." He grinned as he watched her tramp along through the grass with her head high and her hair bobbing on top of her head.

He liked the idea of Heather cutting his hair. He could imagine how sweet it would be to have her so close. To share a laugh with her and enjoy something so simple. It made him feel good to think of her fussing over him.

"Thanks, Heather. I'd appreciate any-thing you could do to make me more presentable, especially before I officiate at Greg and Maya's wedding."

"I'll do my best. Now it's your turn." She stopped and motioned for him to catch up to her. "Get out there and do *your* best. There are a lot of treasures waiting for us."

"I hope you're right, Heather," he murmured. Then before he started looking too much like a big, love-struck goof, he hustled after her.

He'd almost reached her side when the worn sole of his beat-up old tennis shoe hit a mud slick at the top of the riverbank's downward slope.

"Whoa!" He went skidding, then caught himself.

"Michael!" Heather bounded through the tall grass toward him. "Are you okay?"

"I'm okay!" He held his hand up to reassure everyone, then leaned forward to catch his breath. "Nothing injured but my pride. And since the ministry has pretty much divested me of that, everything's fine."

"Maybe you should take a job by the

cabins, Reverend Garrison!" someone called out.

"Are you kidding?" Another voice joined the good-natured ribbing. "And let him loose around all those ladders, hammers and windows?"

A laugh went up. Michael bowed to acknowledge his less-than-coordinated reputation.

"You really are a great guy, you know that?" Heather beamed at him.

That was the best reward of all.

"Let's start our search down near the water. That's where people are having the best results." She reached out toward him.

He slid his hand into Heather's. He didn't need her help, but he didn't mind accepting it if it meant sharing a few moments hand in hand with her. "I'll try my best not to fall in the river."

"That's okay." She gave his fingers a squeeze. "If you do, I'll jump in to save you."

"You'd do that?" A week ago he suspected she'd rather let him drift away with the current.

"Of course I would. I'd never leave you hanging out there on your own with nothing to cling to. Not like…"

Like who? John Parker? Her father?

Heather let go of his hand then and began to tug on the work gloves she had been carrying.

Apparently, she didn't think she needed to name names.

"Okay, so I guess you need to work with me along the river." She motioned him along with a wave of her arm.

He hustled down the slope and waded into the knee-high weeds and prairie grass. "You've gotten a lot done out here in the last few days. Your dad would be proud."

"I doubt that. Nothing I did ever got his attention, much less made him proud." She walked slowly, placing each footfall with care as she used her gloved hand to brush the overgrowth from side to side.

Michael mimicked her actions, his head down, his eyes scanning the ground for anything worth saving. "Over the years, as people learned about what was in that report, they never thought any less of you. Many had issues with Edward. I had hoped you and Edward made peace before he died."

"We did, I think." She paused, looked up, then sighed. "I tried my best. Even after a lifetime of his pushing me away, I took care of him to the very end."

"I wish I'd known he was ill. I'd have gladly come to minister to him."

"He had his own local minister, though I think he would have liked to have seen you. He always had a soft spot for you, I think. Unlike the way he felt about me." She lowered her gaze, took a step forward, bent down to pick something up, then stood again, empty-handed. "Me, even to the very end I couldn't be the one thing that would have made him love me. I couldn't be his own flesh and blood."

Michael wanted to go to her. To take her in his arms and tell her…what? That not only had he had a crush on her as a kid, but that he had always loved her?

They seemed to have mended a lot of fences in the last couple of days, but if he professed that he still loved her she'd probably *push* him in the river and let him flounder.

He couldn't fix her past relationship with her father. And it was way too soon to talk to her about any potential relationship for the two of them in the future. He could only deal with this moment, this time they were sharing here and now.

"So." He whacked at a tall patch of weeds in his way. Change of subject. That was in order. "Avery found a picture frame and a few knickknacks. How about you?"

Heather paused, gazed at the river flowing past and crinkled her nose. "I've spent most of the time supervising painters and fix-ups at the cottages."

"So you've found…?"

"Zip." She raised her hand, her thumb and forefinger forming a circle.

Now here was news he could use. "Great. Then how 'bout you and I have a little contest? First one to find something of value buys the other one lunch."

She cocked her head and pursed her lips. "The town is supplying lunch."

"Excuses, excuses. You scared you won't find anything?"

She looked at the cottages, then at him. Her eyes held a sadness that clutched at his heart.

"Because I know *I* will," he said with still, sure power.

"Will what?" she wanted to know.

"Find something of immeasurable worth." He put his hands on his hips and narrowed one eye to help him focus on her face in the brilliant sunshine. "In fact, I'm looking at something right now."

Heather whipped her head around to look behind her. "What? Where? You see something of value?"

"Yeah. I see the most valuable thing in the world." He lowered his voice. "I see a friend."

She was visibly moved for the briefest moment before she narrowed her eyes at him, tipped up her nose and said, "If you think you're going to weasel out of this challenge that easily, you have another think coming."

"Me? Weasel?" He stabbed his thumb against his breastbone. "I'm the one who suggested the contest! Not to mention that I am an ordained minister of the Gospel. And, if I recall correctly, in that line of work there is no weaseling allowed."

"Big talk." She laughed and held up her hands. "From someone well on his way to owing me lunch served on a blanket picnic-style by the water's edge. Deal?" She thrust out her hand. "If you find more things, I will serve you lunch and if I find more things—"

"You come to church Sunday and hear me preach."

Heather inhaled through her teeth and withdrew her hand. She swept her way-ward hair back in place as she said, gingerly, "Sunday is a bad day for me."

He couldn't believe she was fighting him on this. "Sunday is the only day I preach."

"I mean *this* Sunday is bad for me. I have a packed schedule going around to other churches, to after-church activities, Sunday School classes, Youth Groups and even a church board meeting called especially for my benefit so that I can talk to people about what Helping Hands is doing in High Plains and how they can do their parts."

"Fair enough." This time he put out his hand. He had here and now wrapped up. His next goal was to get her to commit to hanging around a little longer. "What about the Sunday after next?"

She interlaced her work-gloved fingers and wiggled them. "I can't promise that. I do have a lot of work waiting for me in Wichita, you know."

"Work?" Her choice of words intrigued him. "Not, I have 'a life waiting for me' or 'someone special waiting for me'?"

"Okay. If I find more things, you serve me lunch. If you find more things, I'll hear you preach. *If* you find more things." She slipped her work glove off her right hand.

"Deal." He reached out.

"Deal." She whispered it this time as she

fit her hand easily into his, then added breathlessly, "And, Michael?"

Her voice tripped over his raw nerves like a cool breeze over his sweat-dampened neck. "Yeah, Heather?"

"Don't fall in the river." She gave him a light shove before she spun around to begin her search. "Because now that there's a challenge in the air I might not be as inclined to jump to your rescue."

Chapter Twelve

Heather swept aside and kicked through the grass and weeds much faster than she probably should have, but she couldn't help it. She had to press on, keep moving, put some distance between her and Michael. Besides, she reasoned, she wasn't moving any faster than the quick, erratic beating of her suddenly elated heart.

Had she just promised, even conditionally, not just to stay in High Plains but to go into the sanctuary that held so many painful memories and hear the man tied to those memories preach? What had she been thinking?

She pressed her lips together and tried to force her mind to focus on the task. *Things. Find things. Look.*

Look…at…Michael.

She stole a peek behind her just as he straightened up from examining something close to the ground. Sunlight caught the tips of his tousled hair and bits of grass clung to the tumbles of dark waves. He grinned at her and held something up.

"Muddy hat with a hole in it doesn't count, does it?" He poked his fingers through the giant gaping tear in the blue-and-red baseball cap and wriggled them.

"Not unless you know the fellow with a hole in his head to match!" She feigned rapping her knuckles against the side of her head then held out the black plastic garbage bag she had attached to her belt. "I think we can pitch that."

He grabbed the brim between his thumb and fingers, cocked back his arm and sent it flying, the way a kid might do to skim a flat stone over a still pond. But instead of zinging fast and low to her, the battered cap fluttered up high, got snagged by the wind and fell limply at his feet.

Heather giggled but resisted the urge to tease him about his lack of athletic ability.

"Here." She took a step toward him and bent down.

"No, I can get—"

A sudden blinding pain shot through her head from the point of impact with Michael's forehead.

"Ow!" Michael put his hand on his temple and squeezed his eyes shut. "I always knew you were hardheaded, Heather Duster, but I had no idea your head was pure titanium."

"A metal skull? That would explain the ringing I'm hearing." She stood straight. Keeping her neck bent, she pressed the heel of her hand to the spot just above her eye where they had made contact.

The position of her arm cast a shadow across her line of vision and in that shadow something caught Heather's attention.

He blinked a few times then grinned at her. "I'm seeing stars here. You?"

"Nope. Better." She squinted, trying not to give away what she thought she had discovered until she knew for sure.

"Better? Better than stars?" He took the cap, which he had managed to snatch despite their collision, and peered at her with one eye through the hole. "What? Chirpy little bluebirds?"

"Nope. I'm looking at the first found object of our collecting challenge. And it sparkles, too." Heather bent down and plucked up the delicate locket she'd glimpsed in a tangle of dead grass and leaves.

"What is it?"

She let the small locket dangle from her fingers for a moment to show him, then tucked it away in her shirt pocket and gave it a pat. "That's one find for me."

He looked a little stunned and a little amused and actually more than a little pleased…though she didn't dare imagine what he found so pleasant. Being with her? Enjoying their challenge? Knowing that no matter who found the most things, the end result would be that they helped people and would be spending more time together?

Or maybe…

Heather shut her eyes. Avery was right. She did overthink things.

So instead of trying to read too much into Michael's expression, she grabbed the hat and popped it in the trash sack. "If you want to catch up, you'd better stop playing around and get hunting."

She spun around, took a step and almost tripped over something.

"I am not playing around. I'm being thorough. The Bible says seek and ye shall find."

"Ha! Thorough? Is that what you want me to believe? You always wanted to wait until everything was just right before you'd take action. And here I wasn't even *seeking* just now and look what I found!" She pried up the brown leather, mud-caked mass and held it aloft.

He squinted. "What is it?"

She held it an arm's length away from her body and gave it a shake to try to dislodge some of the dirt and any potential "guests" such as worms or bugs. "I know it's been a long time, but even Take-A-Hike Mike should recognize a baseball glove when he sees one!"

He peered close, then nodded. "Any identifying marks? Initials? Name?"

Heather shook her head. "Not that I can see just now. It's pretty filthy."

"Don't worry. The volunteers working with the lost and found will get it cleaned up before Greg adds it to the online catalog."

"It's all working together so well, isn't it?"

"Why shouldn't it? It's High Plains. We don't just share a zip code. We share a history."

Heather stood there on the riverbank and looked around her. The cottages. The townspeople. Michael. *They* shared a history.

Her? She was the girl not good enough to marry John Parker. The girl who did not even know who her father was. Not good enough to win the love of the man who had raised her.

How could she ever hope to belong anywhere? Least of all here?

"Hey, Heather, this time I've really found something." Michael's warm voice called her back from her moment of doubt and melancholy

"What?" She wrapped the baseball glove in the garbage sack that only had the cap in it, to keep it from getting mud and dirt everywhere, then turned to Michael. "A broken—"

Michael stood no more than two feet away, holding a single purple flower between his thumb and forefinger.

He raised his gaze to hers over the petals trembling in the breeze.

Never let them see you cry. She had always equated that with not showing weakness, with always wanting to put on a brave face to protect herself. Not once in all those years that she had made that her motto did she consider that it might apply to the sweet swelling of emotion she now felt.

She sniffled.

Michael smiled and held the flower out,

seeming almost tentative as he waited for her to accept the offering.

A shimmer of unshed tears blurred her vision. She smiled and took the flower.

"Lunch is ready!" Avery practically bounced down the slope of the river toward them.

"Thank you for the flower," she whispered.

Michael put his hand on her back as he urged her with him up the bank. "We can put it in a plastic cup and use it to decorate the picnic blanket when I serve you that picnic lunch for winning one challenge."

"You two won't believe all the stuff people have brought in. My hands got cramped from writing everything down." Avery, in her overalls and a High Plains High School T-shirt, crooked then straightened her fingers. She wasn't just smiling, she was beaming with pride at what she had accomplished.

"After all the work you did on the cottages this morning?" Heather called out. She let Michael help her up the riverbank—not because she needed the help but because she liked having him help her, and she wanted to make sure she didn't smoosh the flower he'd given her. "I think more than your fingers will be sore."

"I'm all right." Avery waved off any concern, then pivoted to run back to where they were serving lunch, calling back, "In fact, I feel so good I may go door to door later handing out flyers for Tommy's lost dog."

Michael took the garbage sack from Heather, tossed it into the grass then took her hand. "Thank you for helping with Avery. It's really made a difference."

Making a difference. That's what she had wanted when she started Helping Hands Christian Charity. Now all she seemed to do anymore was paperwork, appeasing people and chasing down donors.

"Thank you, Michael, for giving me the chance to do that," she whispered.

She raised her face to feel the sun on her cheeks and couldn't help seeing all the people who had come out to work on what was now her property. They laughed and chatted and shared their burdens as readily as they shared their meals.

The sight filled Heather with a kind of purpose and satisfaction she had not known in years. "Thank you for giving me back a little piece of my personal history."

He helped her the rest of the way up with a sure but subtle pull on her arm. When she reached his side, he steadied her by cupping her elbow in his hand, careful of the flower in her hand.

Heather held her breath, standing there so close to him she could see the darkness of his pupils opening against the blue of his eyes.

"If there's anything else I can do, anything else I can give you, Heather." He leaned in even closer. "Just ask."

Tell me that I am not unlovable. Tell me that you will always trust me with the truth, even if the truth isn't pretty. Heather thought of all the things she might ask of him and then of the one thing he had asked of her. To stay long enough to hear him preach.

She owed it to him to stick around long enough not only to help the town she loved, but also to find the courage to go into the sanctuary at High Plains Christian Church.

"You've done enough for me, Michael, just by being yourself, just by being my friend." She moved past him. "I think it may be time I ask what I still have to do for myself."

Chapter Thirteen

Michael had kept his sermons brief since the storm. For starters, he had had so little time to dedicate to preparation and, more important, as the weeks went on he found himself less sure of what to tell people to give them succor anymore. In the long run, he felt people needed fellowship. So he encouraged them to spend more time during the morning greeting actually greeting one another, not just asking "How are you?" but also listening to the answer.

This Sunday, he had spent the time not just listening but also looking at the door, hoping against hope that Heather would walk through.

But the service came and went and Michael did not see Heather. That had to have taken a real effort on her part, since High Plains was a small town and he'd really wanted to run into her.

He'd gone out for coffee and dessert with members of his congregation at Elmira's Pie Diner. Later, while Avery pitched in helping the local veterinarian, Lexi Harmon, clean pens and do general maintenance for the many animals left homeless by the storm, he had made house calls to the injured or elderly who had not been able to attend services. That meant he covered most of the town by the time he headed back to the parsonage with Avery to host the Youth Group Bible Study that evening. All without once crossing paths with Heather Waters.

He did not take it personally. She'd told him she'd be at another church that morning, but he imagined she could have rescheduled if she'd really wanted to. Deep down he knew it wasn't him she was avoiding, but his church. Specifically, the sanctuary of his church.

He understood her misgivings, of course. And he knew that, given time, he could overcome them. *Given time.*

He pushed open the door to his home and flipped on the light.

There was no guarantee that Heather would stick around long enough to change her mind. So Michael would have to change it for her. And while he was at it, if he could get her to fall in love with him…

"I'm going to check the answering machine." Avery shot past him. "I haven't heard from my best friend back home all week. I sent her a text and told her I'd be home today and she should call."

Michael tensed. He hadn't told Avery the news about her friend, or let her know that her own mother thought she should stay in High Plains for at least one semester. On one hand he hated keeping anything from the kid, but on the other?

He was more than a little angry with his

sister for abdicating her role in this particular situation. He couldn't help but wonder if part of the reason Avery had gotten so out of control was that his sister and her husband were more concerned about having their child like them than having her respect them. They always wanted to play the good guys, to be friends with their only child. They never wanted to risk her getting angry with them or harboring any negative feelings toward them at all. In doing so, they had cultivated in Avery the very things they had gone to great lengths to avoid—disrespect for them and any rules they later tried to enforce.

In waiting to tell Avery the news about their plans, Michael had actually been giving his sister time to step up and do the right thing—to be the parent Avery needed her to be.

"Cool! The light is flashing." Her excited voice carried through the still-swinging door that led into the kitchen. "There's a message."

He also had expected that Avery's friend

would contact her, and he wanted to give Avery the opportunity to show her maturity and to recognize his role in guiding her by coming to him with the news, trusting him with her problem.

Beep.

You have...one...new message. The mechanical voice droned out instructions for retrieval as Michael bowed his head to say a prayer for the insight and compassion he would need to handle whatever happened next.

If that message was not from his sister or from Avery's friend, Michael recognized that he'd have to be the one to talk with his niece.

"It's not from her!" Avery called out. "I'll write down the info. Then I'm going to start getting things ready for the meeting."

"Great. Thanks." He'd tell Avery after the wedding ceremony for Greg and Maya tomorrow, he decided. Avery was in a good mood tonight and they still had the Youth Group meeting ahead of them. Why threaten that?

John Parker would have called him

chicken for not pressing the issue. Maybe he was. He shook his head. But why would he even care what a guy he hadn't seen in a decade—who had dealt with his own issues in the most cowardly way imaginable—thought?

He did care, though. Because he feared, deep down, that John might be right. Or that Heather was.

Doing things in God's time doesn't always mean waiting. Sometimes, Take-A-Hike Mike, God's time is now.

He'd rather apply that choice piece of advice to getting Heather to fall for him than to delivering unwelcome news to a fourteen-year-old. If only he had some reason to believe that Heather had moved past whatever it was she had been holding against him all these years. If only she would commit to sticking around long enough for—

"Hello?" A light tapping on the open front door jerked Michael out of his musings. "I'm here. I'm ready. You have me for as long as you need me."

"Heather?" Heather was standing in his doorway looking hot, tired, a bit harried and absolutely beautiful. "What are you doing here?"

"Last stop on my whirlwind tour of the High Plains, Kansas, Sunday meeting speaker's circuit." She gathered her hair in one hand and flipped it up off her neck. "Am I early or can I come on in?"

"Yes." He stepped aside to allow her into his living room.

"Yes? Yes to which?" She came in laughing, her hair still upswept in one hand. "Because if I'm early—"

"You are, by about a half hour, but I don't mind. Come on in. Sit down. Make yourself…" He almost said *comfortable,* but given her long day and his hand-me-down furniture that might be asking too much. Besides, comfort meant very little to Heather. Edward Waters had afforded her every comfort money could buy and that had not made her happy, nor had she been shallow enough to mistake that for genuinely caring about her. "Make yourself at home."

"If you don't mind letting me crash for a half an hour." She moved to the green faux-leather wingback chair, stared at it then moved past it to plunk down on an overstuffed old couch.

"I don't mind." Michael smiled, shut the door then headed for the other side of that couch. "I don't mind one bit."

Half an hour wasn't much time in the grand scheme of making the woman he had always loved return his affections, but it was a start. And Michael intended to make the most of every minute.

"You just relax," he told her as he plopped down beside her. "Hungry? You want something cool to drink? Avery is in the kitchen she can—"

"Uncle Michael, do you know a guy named…" The kitchen door swung open so hard it banged against the wall. Avery stood on the threshold with a broad smile on her face and a piece of paper in her hand. "Hey, Heather! What are you doing here?"

"She's going to say a few words to the Youth Group," Michael explained.

"Cool! She going to tell us what you were like when you were a kid?" Avery's eyes gleamed in good humor. "You know, inspire us by saying no matter how goofy we are now there's still hope we can turn out okay?"

Michael didn't know whether to feel defensive that his niece called his younger self *goofy* or to take pride in her saying aloud that he had turned out "okay." High praise from a girl who hadn't wanted to come to stay with him.

"I'm going to talk about Helping Hands and ask your friends to get the word out about our services, both for people who need them and for people who might want to volunteer," Heather chimed in before Michael could formulate a response to the girl's words.

"They're not really my friends," Avery shot back. "They're just the kids who go to Uncle Michael's church. My real friends wouldn't be caught dead here."

Condescending? Dismissive? Michael tried to pick up any subtle messages in her tone or read something into the way her shoulder sagged against the open door. Did she feel sorry for those old friends? Was she voicing contempt for the hayseeds who would spend a Sunday evening at a Youth Group meeting? Maybe she was just feeling lonely, missing her old friends, still not really sure of the new ones.

Under other circumstances Michael might have explored all that with a question or two. But he didn't think the girl needed that kind of pressure in front of Heather or with the group set to arrive before too long.

So he leaned forward on the couch and rested his forearms on his knees. He'd decided to wait to deal with Avery and he'd stick to that plan. Not to mention the plan he had for making a connection with Heather. "Why don't you go get Heather a cold drink while I keep her company out here."

"Keep her company?" Avery crinkled up her nose, then her whole face brightened. "Oh, I get it. Make yourself scarce, kid, the 'just friends'—" she curled the paper in her hand into a ball while she made invisible quotation marks in the air with her fingers "—want to be alone. You know, just 'friend' stuff. 'Cause you're such good 'friends' and all."

The paper in her hand crinkled. Her fingers were getting a real workout, as was her smile, which she couldn't seem to get under control.

Michael could hardly hold that against her. He was feeling a bit like a grinning idiot himself as he looked at the woman next to him and felt like nothing now would stand in the way of their friendship blossoming into so much more.

"Drinks, please, Avery?" he prodded his niece.

"Okay, but I'm just doing it because you're not the only ones glad to see you guys being friends again," she teased. She turned to go back to the kitchen then froze and gazed down at the piece of paper in her hand. "Oh, wait. Speaking of friends. Someone who said he was a friend of yours called."

"Yeah? Who?" Michael asked when what he really wanted to say was, leave the note and I'll get to it later.

Avery glanced down at the paper. "Do you remember a John Parker?"

"John?" Heather scooted to the edge of the couch.

"What does he want?" Michael asked flatly.

"He wants to make a *huge* donation to the town but he said he wants to make sure his money only goes to—" she held up the piece of paper and read from it word for word "—a legitimate nonprofit, IRS-recognized charity."

Michael and Heather glanced at each other. Heather scowled then looked away, clearly troubled.

"He plans to do some research, look into Helping Hands—"

"Which he will find in perfect order," Heather snapped.

Avery didn't miss a beat as she finished reading from the note she had written from John's phone message. "And he will be in High Plains to hand over the check next weekend."

"Next weekend?" Heather whispered. "John is coming here next weekend?"

So much for his plans, Michael thought as he watched Heather's face go pale and her expression waver between sadness and panic.

"Is that big news?" Avery wondered aloud as she bounded along toward the kitchen again.

"Heather?" Michael reached out to take her hand but she stood up and moved away. "Are you okay?"

"Fine." She frowned then took a deep breath and straightened her shoulders, her face now almost serene. "I'm fine."

"Oh wow! I just figured it out." Avery gaped at the paper in her hand. "John Parker! That's the cutie in the yearbook! The guy you were going to marry, Heather!"

"We know that," Michael said, trying to come off firm with the girl but not to snap at her.

"Boy, do I ever know it," Heather murmured.

"So what does that mean? Why is he coming here now? I'll bet he got one of the mass e-mails we sent with requests for donations. It mentioned both of you by name." Avery spun around and headed for the kitchen door. "You guys want to listen to the message yourselves and see if you hear something—"

"Stop it, Avery!" Michael rubbed his fingertips against his temples, took a breath then looked at the girl, composed and kind. "I'm sorry. Let's just not make a bigger deal out of this than it's worth, okay?"

Avery's eyes flashed with angry embarrassment. "I just gave y'all the message. Heather is the one running away."

"She's not running away," Michael said. Then he looked at Heather, his heart in his throat. "Are you?"

She shook her head. "It's just been such a long day, and now this little bombshell. I feel drained all of a sudden."

"Go home and rest, then." He moved

around the couch, motioning for her to come on around so he could walk her to the door. "I'll talk to the group about Helping Hands."

"I should do that."

"I can." Avery stepped up, her mood shifting as fast as…well, as fast as a teenager having a mood shift. "I know all the details. Let me do it, Heather."

"Let Avery do it," he urged. He slid his hand across the center of her back, hoping it might lend some physical support to go with the emotional and even spiritual support he hoped she felt from him. "Take care of yourself. Get a good night's sleep so you can see the world through fresh eyes tomorrow. You're invited to Greg and Maya's wedding, you know."

"Wedding?" Her head jerked up. She looked toward the closed door to his study for a moment before she turned to him and whispered, "Michael, I can't attend a wedding in that sanctuary, not knowing that I'm probably going to run into John in a few days. I just can't."

"I know." He had really wanted her

there, not just because he liked the idea of her seeing him officiate, but mostly because he knew that if she could attend then she'd be well on her way to healing for good. "But maybe you can stop by the church to congratulate the happy couple."

"I'll try." She nodded, squared her shoulders and headed for the door. "Thanks, you guys."

"Anytime." He kept his hand on her back, when what he really wanted to do was lean in and give her a kiss. Would she allow him to do that? He thought she just might, but he couldn't tell for sure. He didn't dare guess and risk having her run off again. "I mean that. If you want to talk later, call. I'll be here."

"I don't doubt that." She put her hand on his cheek. "Do you really think John will come back to High Plains?"

"I don't know." Reining in the impulse to kiss her palm, he shook his head, knowing his five o'clock shadow would tickle her instead.

She withdrew, which was for the best.

Michael sighed. "I don't know John anymore."

She folded her hand high against her chest and gazed at him. "I wonder if either of us ever really did."

He raised his shoulder, cocked his head and opened his mouth to say something, though he wasn't sure just what.

It didn't matter. Before he got a sound out Heather grazed his cheek with a quick, sweet kiss then stood back and waved to Avery.

"See you at the wedding tomorrow?" Avery asked.

Heather smiled but did not commit.

Avery gave a wave and slipped into the kitchen.

"She's doing great." Heather went to the door and opened it before looking back. "All things considered."

"I could say the same about you," he said.

"I'll be okay," she assured him, then she brushed his hair out of his eyes and smiled.

He wanted to kiss her but that was not something a minister could do, not right there on his doorstep. Besides, he *always* wanted to kiss her. And there would be other opportunities.

He believed that, even as he watched her walk away knowing that once again, after all these years, Heather had John Parker, not him, on her mind.

Chapter Fourteen

Heather went to her workstation Monday morning and slid her laptop into place.

John Parker was coming back to High Plains. She'd worn herself out yesterday and so had been mostly able to put it out of her thoughts long enough to fall into a deep, if troubled, sleep. This morning, walking through the doors of High Plains Christian Church, the reality of the news came rushing at her in emotions and images that she couldn't quite sort out and identify.

The fund-raising maven in Heather wanted to celebrate John's potential donation as a much-needed and much-appreciated coup. The young left-at-the-altar bride in her should have been furious, anxious, afraid, indignant, perhaps even vengeful. Her woman's heart felt a flutter of excitement at seeing the man again, and at having him see her, see what she had made of herself.

As a Christian, she knew she should reject pretty much all those inclinations. Prideful. Lacking in peace. Shortsighted.

Heather stood on the stage and considered her emotional state. Nothing. No pride. No fear. No craving for revenge or vindication.

Heather felt no special gratitude for John's generosity. Writing a check for a guy like that really meant little more than a tax break and another accolade. As to seeing him again?

She clicked through her e-mails and sent them each to the right files. Nothing that needed her attention at the moment. Heather leaned back in her chair.

"You okay?" Michael stood in the doorway, his head tilted down just enough so that his gaze fixed on her in a sweet but sly way that sent a shiver over her whole body.

Seeing John again, or having him see her, just seemed like the least interesting thing going on in her life right now.

"I'm fine." She flashed a smile that felt a little too quick, a little too tight.

"Heather…" He came into the Fellowship Hall.

"No. Really. Fine." She closed out the screen with her e-mail on it, then turned her attention to straightening stacks of intake forms on the table. "Avery and the volunteers have everything under control in the fund-raising department. I found a couple of locals while making speeches yesterday who really could use a little extra money. So they're going through a crash course taught by none other than Mr. Paisley."

"He actually came back to town?"

"No, they had to go to Manhattan. He really is a great guy. We've used him for work before." She came down the steps and headed across the highly polished part-time Fellowship Hall and part-time gymnasium floor. The sharp striking of her heels resounding through the room echoed her heartbeat. Realizing that, she stopped, leaned her hip against the lost-and-found table and took a deep, calming breath. "I should have a temp staff ready to help people fill out request-for-aid forms starting tomorrow."

"That's good news." He kept walking toward her. "I'm glad you found a way to give the work to people who need it."

"Well, we don't pay a lot but—"

He came to her side, shaking his head. "It's not the money, Heather. You know that money doesn't make you happy. It's about having a sense of purpose. It's about getting involved in something bigger than yourself."

She smiled at the reference and nodded. She stole a quick look at him, decked out in his best clothes, obviously dressed for the wedding that would take place in the church within the next few hours. In the time since she had come back, she'd seen Michael pretty much as a mature version of the young man she had smacked with a wedding bouquet on her own failed wedding day. But now, seeing him looking so strong, confident and handsome in his black suit, white shirt and a blue-and-silver tie that reflected his vivid blue eyes, she felt as though she were looking at a whole new man.

That thrilled and humbled her. She liked the man Michael had become, but found herself wondering. Could he say the same about the director of Helping Hands Christian Charity?

"Something bigger than yourself," she whispered. "I think in a lot of ways that's what's been missing in my own life of late. I've let the bigness of what I've gotten involved with overwhelm me. I forgot the joy that comes from getting your hands dirty, from serving by meeting people in the place where they have the most need."

"Well, if it's dirty hands that make you happy, you have come to the right place, lady." He reached out and ran his fingertip along the lost-and-found table and held the results for her to appreciate.

Heather looked at the dark smudge on

his finger then at those gorgeous eyes. Her heartbeat picked up again. "Actually, everything here seems pretty much under control. Maybe I should see if I can be of help elsewhere."

"*Else*where? *Where* elsewhere?" He rubbed his hands together to clear off the dust.

"Oh. You know, around town." She took a step backward and bumped against the table. "There's still that engagement ring to find. And, um, the mystery surrounding that little girl found after the storm."

"Kasey." He gave the name they had taken to calling the toddler who had only the initials *K.C.* to identify her. "I guess this means you're not attending the wedding today."

"I…" How could she sit in that sanctuary and watch Michael officiate when she had such conflicting emotions about the place and the man? Especially the man.

He was her friend. He had betrayed her. She wanted to forgive him. "I want to…"

"What, Heather? *What* do you want?"

That was the question, wasn't it? What did she want? And how could she find the courage to let go of the things that kept her from it, to become a part of something not just bigger but better than the life she currently had?

"I'm not exactly sure, Michael." She took his hand in hers and gave it a squeeze. "But I'll give it some thought and be back when I have an answer."

"I'll be here," he said softly.

Heather checked the time on her cell phone.

"If you need to be somewhere, I am perfectly capable of handling this from here on out." Officer Colt Ridgeway flipped up a page from the stack of papers on the clipboard in front of him.

Heather had placed some phone calls, put him in touch with people who had all manner of state and federal resources at their disposal and would be happy to offer recommendations. They'd spent the last few hours making calls and downloading information, but hadn't really made any tangible progress in solving the mystery of the sweet little girl the town now called Kasey.

"I hate to leave a job unfinished," she said, then bit her lower lip to keep from blurting out, "But I've already stayed too long."

She'd probably missed the bride going down the aisle. At least she hoped she'd missed that. In the time it would take her to get to the church, the vows would be said. If she timed it right, she'd arrive just as Michael pronounced Greg and Maya husband and wife.

They'd kiss.

Michael would look up. His gaze would meet hers. And then…

Then she'd think of that awful day when Michael had allowed her to walk down that aisle and have her shattered world handed to her by a stranger. But *that* Michael and the one at the church—the minister—were not one and the same.

Trust me. The words drifted to her through the haze of her musings and memories.

"I want to trust you," she murmured then started at her own voice.

"Trust me," Colt was saying. "I've handled every aspect of this investigation so far. I can manage this without supervision."

"Supervision?" Heather cringed.

Colt had said it with a smile, well, the suggestion of a smile, on his lips, but it served to remind Heather that she'd been hovering. "Guess I can't put it off any longer. I'd better get over to the church."

"That sounds like something *I'd* say." He let the page drop, pressed the clipboard to his chest and crossed his arms over it. "I figured *you'd* be glad to go to the church whenever you could."

She let her smile ease slowly over her face. "Because I run a Christian aid organization?"

"Yeah. Sure." He narrowed his eyes at her. "That, and because I've seen the way you and the reverend look at each other."

Her easy smile froze in a brittle grin. "Michael and I are old friends, that's all."

"Lady, this town is full of people I think

of as old friends. I have *never* looked at one of them the way Michael Garrison looks at you." The tall, blond man in uniform barked out a laugh, then lowered his gaze and shook his head. "In other words the good Reverend Garrison has it bad for you."

Michael had asked her what she wanted and she had said she would think about it. But the instant Colt Ridgeway said it out loud, she didn't have to think. She wanted to see that look on Michael's face again.

She didn't care about John Parker. Over all these years, she had hardly given him a thought, other than to reaffirm Edward Waters's assessment that she was not good enough to deserve the love of a good man or to be part of a decent family.

Edward, John and the Parkers were wrong. She *was* worthy of love, and Michael—the good Reverend Garrison— was the man to prove it. Now she just had to go to him and let him know that she returned those feelings.

A few minutes later, Heather climbed out of her car in the parking lot of High

Plains Christian Church. She must have been lost in thought because she didn't even notice the car with the engine running and *Just Married* scrawled in glass chalk across the back window until Avery came running toward her from the direction of the Parish House.

"Hey, Heather, look what I have! Maya let me bring it out here for her so Layla wouldn't get into it while she changed. When Maya gets out here she's going to throw it." Avery hoisted a beautiful wedding bouquet high in the air.

"Careful with that around Heather." Michael, walking only a few steps behind his niece, feigned ducking and covering his head. "She can turn those flowers into a weapon."

"I suppose I should apologize for that." Heather leaned against the fender of her SUV and put one hand on her hip. "It was a childish thing to do. But I've grown up a lot since then."

"We both have." Michael came up close enough to be able to practically whisper and still speak so that his deep, kind voice tripped over her jangled nerves. He stood there and looked at her.

Colt Ridgeway was right. It was not the look from one old friend to another.

"Stand right there. There's only you and me and a couple of Maya's friends who are eligible to catch this thing, so you have to be ready to defend your spot," Avery assured her, as the young teen went up on tiptoe with her eye on the back door of the church, waiting for the wedding party to appear.

Heather drew in a deep breath, catching a whiff of the lush aroma of the flowers opening to the warmth of the sun. She wanted to shut her eyes. To close out even the prospect of trying to catch that bouquet, but she didn't want to miss seeing Maya and Greg in their moment of happiness. She might not have been able to go into the sanctuary and witness the actual ceremony, but she did not want to miss this.

Seconds later the back door opened and people began to come out. Heather recognized Jesse Logan. She didn't know the other young woman who came to stand beside Avery to await the big bridal bouquet toss, but she did know that she did not want to be standing this close to anyone who wanted to be considered for that honor.

She started to step aside, but before she could move Greg came out holding Maya's hand. He looked so tall and handsome, and she the picture of contentment and joy in her understated pale dress and a simple rhinestone headband in her short dark hair.

"They look…like a family."

"They are."

Michael stood behind her so close that she could not have backed away and run now if she had wanted to. She did not want to.

Avery made a mad dash to hand Maya the bouquet, pausing to whisper something in the glowing bride's ear.

"There are still a few legalities," Michael said. "But God has joined them together—all of them—and that's a forever kind of deal."

"A forever kind of deal," Heather

murmured as her heart soared. That's what she wanted. That's what she had always wanted. She started to turn toward Michael to tell him just that when an almost violent tug on her arm yanked her back around.

"She's going to throw it now. Heads up." Avery raised her hands.

The other young woman did, as well.

Heather laced her arms resolutely in front of herself.

"That a girl, Heather Duster," Michael teased. "You never could catch worth beans, anyway."

"I could catch every bit as well as you." She whipped her head around to tell him. Then, to prove it, she turned toward the bride, lifted her arms just as Maya threw the beautiful bundle of pink roses and greenery into the air and the other two girls parted and dropped their hands to their sides. The bouquet tumbled high in the air and into Heather's open hands.

"Yes!" Avery jumped up with one fist held high in triumph at the success of her plan.

Maya laughed and waved, calling, "You're next."

Greg pointed at her. No, not at her. He was pointing directly at his cousin, Michael. He didn't say a word but he didn't have to. The way Michael grinned broadly at her said it all.

The wedding party called out their thanks and goodbyes and climbed into the car. The rest of the gathering moved to their own cars, as well. When only Heather, Avery and Michael remained in the lot, she turned and gazed at him over the richly scented bouquet.

He did not flinch. "Great catch."

"I am beginning to think just that." Heather knew the answer to Michael's question of what she wanted. She pressed her lips together, rallied her courage then finished her thought. "Michael, I have an answer to your question about what I want now."

He went still, as if he had just gotten a message he'd been waiting a long time to hear and couldn't quite believe it. "I'm listening."

Heather took in a deep breath.

"You like the way I set it up so you'd catch the bouquet? Huh, Heather?" Avery squirmed in between Michael and Heather and elbowed Heather. "When you didn't show up for the wedding I thought you'd miss that part, too."

"Sorry, I was late. I got…" She looked up into Michael's blue eyes and murmured, "Sidetracked."

"That's okay. If you hadn't shown up I'd have tried to catch it myself. It's stupid, I know. But…"

"You want it?" Heather looked down at the girl. She'd shown so little interest in things like this quaint family moment, Heather hated for her not to have something to remember it by. She extended the bouquet. "Why don't you have it? I don't have anywhere to keep it, anyway."

"Thanks!" Avery tipped her face down over the small bundle of pink roses, baby's breath and greenery, closed her eyes and inhaled. "This will be cool to show all my friends when I move back home this weekend. They'll probably still be fresh then."

Move back home? This weekend? Heather pulled her shoulders back and tensed. Obviously, Avery had not taken the news about her friend's trouble and her parents' request that she stay in High Plains seriously. Heather took a step backward, withdrawing from the circle the three of them made.

Suddenly she felt so intrusive. Heather gave Michael an empathetic look to let him know she would follow his lead and leave him to discuss this with Avery in private or stay and offer whatever support she could as he did the right thing.

"That's a great idea." Michael put his hand on Avery's back.

He wasn't going to say anything to her. He was going to let her keep thinking that everything was just fine. Heather's stomach churned as if she'd taken a punch low to the gut.

He gave his niece a gentle push toward the parsonage. "Why don't you go put that in the fridge before the petals begin to wilt?"

"Michael?" Heather clenched her hands into the full fabric of her dress at her sides. Her jaw tightened. She pled with him first with her eyes and then with her words. "Say something."

"This doesn't involve you, Heather. I know what I'm doing."

Avery twisted around.

Michael just waved the girl on, then closed the gap between himself and Heather as he said, "Better get those taken care of, Avery. They won't last long in this heat."

Out of the corner of her eyes, Heather saw the girl shrug then pivot. Her dress shoes crunched on some gravel in the parking lot to sound her retreat.

Heather's retreat was not so precise, but she couldn't help but liken her own heart and dreams to those bits of rock and gravel, crushed under the weight of Michael's deception.

"You were saying?" he prodded as he moved so close she could smell his after-shave and hear the whisper of the fabric of his suit. "Something about knowing what you wanted?"

Never let them see you cry.

Heather choked through the tightening in her throat and scowled to keep the true depths of her pain and disappointment from showing on her face as she stood tall and said, as firmly as she could, "I wanted to tell you how much I thought you had changed. But in light of what I just heard, I realize just how wrong I was about that."

Chapter Fifteen

"When were you going to tell Avery that the things she'd been hoping for, dreaming of, were not going to happen?" Heather turned her back on him, and in doing so faced the back of the parking lot and the High Plains River, which flowed quietly by, constant and impervious to the trials of the people who lived and worked and struggled on its banks. "When were you finally going to tell her the truth? When she had her suitcase packed and was out the door on her way to the car?"

"No. You know better than that, Heather. I planned to tell her when it needed to be done. And by the way, I had my reasons for not telling her sooner, which are my business—mine and my family's."

"Right." She lifted her face and the breeze blew her hair back, making her look regal and righteous and absolutely beautiful. "Because what the high and mighty families in High Plains deem proper and necessary is the only thing that matters, even more than individual people and their feelings."

Michael could not look at her standing there like that and take offense at her attempt to antagonize him. He knew this woman. Knew her history and her heart. And he loved her too much to let her gut reaction to this small piece of his family's drama keep him from saying what needed to be said.

He moved to her side, his own face in the wind and his gaze fixed on the river. "Why do I have a feeling that we're not really talking about Avery here?"

The wind whipped at them. The river rolled on.

Finally, Heather bowed her head slightly and said, "You let me walk down the aisle."

"*Let* you?" Michael looked Heavenward and gave a sharp, acquiescent laugh. "I was just as surprised by John's choice as you were."

"Hardly!" She turned slightly to face him, her hair unfurling in ribbons across her nose and lips as she spoke in a rapid, accusatory growl. "You could have come to me before I made a big fool of myself."

"First, you did not make a fool of yourself." He took her by the shoulders so that he could make eye contact and keep it. After all these years, if they were going to finally hash this out it would be eye-to-eye. "John's actions may have left you feeling foolish, but that was him, not you. If anyone was the big fool, it was him for not standing up to his family and marrying you."

"You were in that sanctuary, Michael. He wasn't."

The naked pain in her eyes kept him from pointing out that that was pretty much what he had said. He did not understand her anger at him when it was John Parker who had been the cad, the jerk, the one who had left her standing there.

"When the minister came to the front of the sanctuary and you realized that John wasn't going to be there, and that I was about to come through those doors, you should have stormed down the aisle and stopped me."

He couldn't deny that, and it grieved him to realize that his poor choice all those years ago had caused Heather so much anguish. "But when I saw you…in your wedding gown, walking toward me…"

For the first time since this conversation had begun, Heather's fury subsided. The tension went out of her shoulders. Her face paled. She blinked and her eyes were moist, though she did not shed a single tear.

"I kept thinking there was no way on earth that John wasn't going to show up and claim you." He reached up and touched her cheek. "I would have."

"But I'm not talking about John." She drew a shuddering breath, then moved away from his touch. "John didn't love me. He chose a really rotten way to let me know that, but in the end we were both better off that he didn't show up that day. I know that now."

He didn't know exactly what to say to that. She was already steamed enough at him over something he couldn't quite grasp. He didn't want to risk making things worse by telling her how relieved he felt to hear her say that. So he put on his best thoughtful-listener expression and said, "I see."

"Do you?" She shook her head. "Because I don't think you do. I don't think you see what this is about at all."

He stroked his thumb over her arm as he tried to chose his words carefully. "It's about…John…and—"

"No! Don't drag John into this. Don't try to make this about him."

Michael dropped his hand to his side and gave it a shake as though it had been burned.

"Don't try to make your nonwedding *to* John when you were jilted *by* John *about* John? Then who should I make it about?"

"This is about you—" she pointed to herself and then him "—and me."

Realizing that her words had not matched her actions, she tried again. "I mean about me—" she pointed to him then to herself "—and you."

He tried not to grin. Sincerely, he tried.

Heather groaned and balled her uncooperative fingers into a fist as she made sweeping circular gestures. "This is about us."

"I thought you were angry about Avery."

"Avery is just an example. Another example of the problem here, which is you, Michael."

"I thought the problem was—" he did an exaggerated imitation of her gesture "—us."

"No. The issue is us. The problem is you." She stabbed her finger in his direction.

"Me? But John…"

"We've gone over that. I've come to terms with the fact that not getting married to him was a good thing. John didn't love me. You, however—"

"Did," he murmured so quietly he knew she didn't even hear him.

"You were my friend, Michael. I thought I would always be able to count on you." Her voice broke with the last few words but she did not let them dissolve into a sob. She fixed her gaze on the river and in the very next breath, rallied and concluded, "And the fact that you don't get that tells me it's an issue that time hasn't healed and will probably never be resolved."

He shook his head. "What does that mean?"

"It means the fact that you withheld the truth from Avery proves to me that you either put your own emotional comfort ahead of other people's pain, which I really do not want to believe of you. Or you still think you know what's best for everyone. Knowing what's best for someone is just another way of saying that someone isn't smart enough or good enough to deserve your honesty."

"What? No. That's not... I never...

Heather, think about what you just said for a minute. Deciding when and where and how I would tell Avery that her folks and I think she should stay in High Plains through at least the end of the year is not—"

A sharp gasp and the churning of gravel underfoot cut him off. He jerked his head up to scan the area around them, behind them. "Avery? Avery!"

"She must have come back out of the house." Heather wadded his suit jacket sleeve in her hand. She, too, craned her neck to search the parking lot and beyond.

"Or was hiding close by to eavesdrop." Given her interest in playing matchmaker between him and Heather, it made sense that she would want to sneak a peek to see if her efforts had come to fruition.

"Would she run away?" Heather asked, her face ashen.

"You're the one who seems to see so much of yourself in her." He pulled his sleeve from her viselike grip and brushed out the wrinkles her damp palm had created. "Tell me, would *you* run away?"

Michael did not wait for her to confirm the answer they both already knew. He turned abruptly and headed toward the parsonage.

"What are you going to do?" Heather called out.

"I'm going to go after her, like I should have done when you ran out of this church all those years ago." He looked back at her, his heart heavy but his thoughts fixed on helping his niece. "I have grown up enough to know that when I make a mistake now, I have to correct it. And the sooner, the better. I never meant to judge you, Heather. I just made a mistake, one I guess I am going to have to live with the rest of my life."

Chapter Sixteen

Michael did not look back as he reached the walkway to the parsonage. His shoulders back and his head high, he still made such a lonely figure, a dark silhouette against the outline of his simple home.

Heather, her heart aching, wanted to call out to him, but she didn't know what she could possibly say. Should she shout out "I want to believe you, but I don't dare" or "You just don't get how badly hurt I have been"? Neither seemed adequate.

Or fair.

She sighed and headed for the church so she could gather a few things from her temporary office. Nothing left for her now but to go home for the day.

Home? Heather's home was not in High Plains. Given what she had just learned, that she could not trust the one man she wanted to trust with her whole heart with something as simple as looking out for a kid's feelings, she knew now it never would be.

That made her pick up her pace toward the church, shoulders back and chin up.

"Avery? I'm sorry about how this has turned out. Let's talk." Compassion, worry and maturity met in Michael's voice as shouted to be heard inside the house as he bounded up the front steps.

He was a good man. Heather could not deny that. Michael really cared about his niece, and clearly he had learned from his past mistakes. As soon as he found Avery he would sort things out, make them right.

But what about her? What about their friendship?

I've seen the way he looks at you. Colt Ridgeway's words echoed in her thoughts.

She put her hand on the rail and her foot on the first step, then looked toward the parsonage.

What about them having more than a friendship? He had let that go so easily. How could she have imagined he could have cared for her like that? No one else ever had.

Just then the scent of roses and fresh greenery filled her senses. She looked down to find a smattering of torn and scattered petals under her feet.

"Avery," she whispered, visually tracing the tattered bits of pink and green up the stairs and into the church. She hesitated for only a heartbeat to consider going to get Michael, then charged up the stairs, through the main doors, the foyer and up to the doors of the sanctuary.

She pressed her palm to the old wood that, through the generations, so many people from High Plains had touched. She shut her eyes and bowed her head in prayer.

"Please, Lord, please, go before me in love. Surround me in Your strength. Let Your wisdom shine through me and may

Your goodness and mercy follow me always," she whispered.

She opened her eyes and in that moment imagined all the hands that had been laid upon this very door over the years. On the happiest of days and the saddest. In times of celebration and commemoration. Bringing every human emotion to lay before the one God who would welcome them into His arms no matter how poor or how ragged, how unloved or unworthy they may have felt themselves to be.

They had all crossed this threshold, just as Heather had on her would-be wedding day. Now she had to do it again. Could she?

A child was hurting, feeling all alone in the world. Heather chose to take her own advice. "Sometimes God's time means you cannot wait."

With that she took a deep breath and pushed open the door.

The sanctuary had changed very little since she had run out of it ten years ago. Sunshine, tinted red and yellow by the stained-glass windows, illuminated the walls. It gave a gleam to the wood of the ceiling, the pews, the pulpit and the softly lit cross on the back wall.

Heather held her breath. Her cheeks flushed. She took a step, faltered then looked down, half expecting the ground to have turned to quicksand. Finding instead the more worn and definitely dustier old maroon carpeting she remembered now littered with more rose petals, she rallied and went farther in.

"Avery?" she whispered.

Nothing.

"I know you're in here. I can see where you've been tearing at the bouquet and dropping leaves and petals." Heather took another step.

No response.

"Your uncle Michael is worried about you."

At last something between a cry and derisive "ha" came from the front row.

Heather hurried forward to find the young girl curled up on her side on the pew, clutching the bouquet the way a younger child might cling to a teddy bear. She approached cautiously.

Avery did not flee or flinch or even raise her head. She just lay there, her shoulders shaking with every gut-wrenching, silent sob.

Heather knelt before the pew and ran her hand over Avery's soft brown hair. "I know. It seems like a boneheaded move on your uncle's part not to tell you about the change of plans right away, but he didn't do it to hurt you."

"I know."

"You *know?*" Heather's hand stilled. She had expected rage and contempt from the girl toward Michael, but this quiet, accepting admission threw her. "Then why did you run away from him?"

"I didn't. I ran… I ran here." She sat up at last and sniffled. "Because Uncle Michael said that if you have God on your side, you will be able to stand up to all the miserable junk in the world that tries to knock you down."

The simplicity of the way the girl had

just encapsulated Michael's whole dedication homily made Heather smile, just a
teeny bit. "That's right."

"Well." The girl swiped her hand under
her nose. "I was knocked down, wasn't I?"

"Yep." Heather nodded. Stroked the
girl's sweat-dampened hair back from her
pale forehead then looked around and
found a box of tissues at the end of the row,
kept there for funerals and weddings and
christenings and perhaps particularly pene-
trating sermons, any time a member of the
congregation might get weepy. She tugged
free a couple of sheets and handed one to
Avery. "You were thrown for a real loop."

"It's not fair. I don't think anything can
help me stand this," she moaned and in the
next breath threw herself, blubbering, into
Heather's arms.

Startled, Heather tensed. Then she remembered her own prayer and the passage
from Ephesians that Michael had quoted
when they dedicated the land to rebuild
the town hall. It seemed only right that
God would bring her back to this sanctu-

ary where she had once run from her own pain and disappointment and give her the chance to do what she had not done before. To stand. She could do this.

"Life isn't always fair, kiddo." She wrapped Avery into a deep, comforting hug. "But you can stand it. You can stand firm in your convictions. But to do that, you may need a little help from your friends here. Like me. Like your uncle Michael."

Avery sniffled and pulled away. "It's good to have friends, but I…I…need… I should be able to count on…my…my…"

The word seem to strangle in her throat.

But Heather did not need to hear the word. She felt it to the very core of her being, felt the girl's pain, and for the first time in her life, gave voice to the stark and brutal truth that she had pushed down for so long.

"Mom." She finished the girl's thought. "You should have been able to count on your mom. And your dad. They should have been the ones to tell you this, no matter what they feared you might think of them afterward."

Saying it aloud seemed to cement everything in Heather's mind. She knew now that the pain she had carried, the anger toward her father, John and especially Michael had been misdirected. The person she should have been able to always trust, who should have always been honest and supportive of her, was her own mother. The fact that her mom had kept the truth from her was the real reason Heather never really felt worthy of being loved.

Why had her own mother not been the one to tell her about her birth father? Even though they had reached their own kind of peace at the end of his life, she had to wonder why Edward hadn't owned up to the truth and helped her cope with it after her mother's death.

Those questions, unasked, had gnawed at Heather and torn her up inside for far too long. Her stubbornness in blaming Michael had allowed her to ignore them. That only served to keep the wounds forever fresh.

"They should have stepped up and laid

it out for you. Good and bad. The whole messy reality of it all," Heather whispered, speaking her own deepest desire as well as confirming what she knew should have happened for Avery.

"Yes!" Avery buried her face in Heather's hair and sobbed.

"*That's* what I was waiting for," came the clear, calm voice of the minister of High Plains Christian Church from the back of the sanctuary. "I wanted to give your folks every chance to handle this the right way, Avery. But I'm done waiting. I just talked to your mom and she and your dad are on their way here to talk this all out with you."

Avery was up and out of the pew so fast the wedding bouquet, or what was left of it, spilled onto the floor at Heather's feet. The girl sniffled. "Really? Are they going to take me home?"

Michael shook his head. "Not if I have my way."

Avery's lower lip quivered.

He cleared his throat and dipped his head as he ran his hand back through his hair.

Heather braced herself for another Take-A-Hike Mike moment, where he'd backtrack and hem and haw and try to get everything just right.

"You've come so far, grown as a young lady and as a Christian, especially since the storm. You have a new sense of purpose and compassion now that went totally uncultivated among your old friends and lifestyle. But that work is far from finished in you." Until that moment he had held Avery's gaze but he lifted it then to Heather, seeming to say—how's that for trusting someone with the truth? "I'd hate to see you slip back into your old habits now."

"I... Okay. I get that." The girl nodded.

"You do?" Michael showed his surprise at that with an amused scowl.

"I don't like it. But I *get* it." Another sniffle before Avery stepped into the aisle and started for the door, her eyes narrowed to slits and her mouth hard.

Michael's eyes followed the girl until she was right in front of him.

She paused.

He tucked his hands in the pockets of his black suit pants and just waited for what Heather expected would be a tirade or a temper tantrum at the very least.

The niece and uncle locked gazes.

Heather stood, wondering if she should say something to break the stalemate.

Avery beat her to it.

"Thank you, Uncle Michael." The girl gave him a hug so tight it almost threw him off balance.

He looked at Heather, puzzled, then a wide grin broke out across his face. "You're welcome. I mean that. You're always welcome to stay with me, Avery. You always have a home in High Plains."

"I know," the girl gurgled into his suit jacket before she pushed upright and angled her chin high. "But I still don't like it."

Michael nodded. "Understood."

With that she headed down the aisle. "I want to change before my folks get here."

"Would it be too obvious for me to tell her she's already changed more than her parents will ever belie—" He swung his head around to face Heather and his whole expression shifted. "Are you… Heather? You're not supposed to be crying now. Everything has worked out."

Heather tipped up her head and met Michael's gaze, unashamed of the tears bathing her eyes and streaming down her cheeks. "Oh, Michael. I am so sorry I judged you so harshly, both as far as Avery was concerned and when we were kids."

"Hey, you always thought of me as Take-A-Hike Mike, the kid who waited so long for the perfect pitch that he never even took a swing. You were right that I should have acted sooner, both with Avery *and* with you and John."

"I had no business accusing you of that. You did what you could, you acted when you knew action was needed. You believed everything would be right in God's time."

"Sometimes God's time means our own agendas have to be put on hold," he reminded her.

Heather gulped back a sob and shook

her head. "I wasted too many years holding you accountable for the shortcomings of John Parker, his family, Edward Waters and even my own mother. Can you ever forgive me?"

"Done," he whispered.

"Really?" She wiped the second tissue she had taken for Avery under her eyes.

"Really," he said, coming to her at last. "Heather, I love you. I have always loved you."

"Oh, Michael, I…I…" Because she couldn't help it, she put the tissue to her nose and blew.

Michael stared at her for only half a second before he burst out laughing. "Is that a 'Get lost you loser' honk or an 'I love you, too' one?"

"The second one." She dabbed the tissue to her nose then lifted her chin and tried to salvage what was left of her dignity and control. Not that she really cared about dignity or control now that she finally had everything she'd ever dreamed of. She was loved.

Just what kind of love Michael meant by that she wasn't sure and for now it did not matter. She and Michael had mended their friendship. They had mended their broken trust. That would create the right foundation for anything else to follow. Knowing that was enough for now.

"I love you right back, Michael. I have always loved you, even when I didn't like you very much." She took a step, then, not quite sure she could walk down the aisle at Michael Garrison's side without reading too much into it, moved past him.

"Hey, you forgot the bou—"

When Michael broke off midword, Heather jerked her head up.

"Hello, Heather. I hope I haven't arrived at a bad time."

Heather froze, unable to do anything but stare at the man with the coal-black hair, broad grin and deep-set brown eyes that never seemed to reveal what was going on inside the man himself.

John Parker. Not just back in High Plains, but walking into the sanctuary where he should have met Heather all those years ago on their would-be wedding day. Her pulse quickened but out of sheer surprise, not because she was excited to see him.

In fact, looking at him she felt very little at all. An old friend. Someone she used to know. Someone she might never see again after this moment and that was perfectly okay with her.

For a second she remembered the first time she saw Michael on the TV the night of the tornado. Her skin tingled. Her cheeks went hot.

For ten years she had ached over leaving this church and now she knew why— because she had left Michael. Just as she had said before, this had nothing to do with John. Seeing him here now only solidified that fact in her mind. And confirmed to her that her love for Michael went way beyond friendship.

"Well, here we are, the Three Amigos back together again."

Michael strode up the aisle and when he reached Heather, handed her the flowers that Maya had tossed to her less than an hour ago. "These are yours, I believe."

John's eyes widened. He looked from Heather in her sundress to Michael in his suit, then up toward the altar still adorned with the unity candle from Greg and Maya's wedding. "No! It can't be! The two of you?"

Heather and Michael looked at one another. Both of them opened their mouths to set John straight, but before they got even a sound of protest out, their old friend had them caught up in a bear hug.

"I am so happy for you guys! I knew all along it was you two who belonged together." He gave them a squeeze.

"We're not—"

"My cousin Greg is the one who just got married." Michael pulled free of his friend's embrace then gave Heather a sly sidelong look as he added, "Heather and I are just…working on finding some common ground."

It wasn't a proposal. It wasn't even commitment. But Michael Garrison had said more with that phrase than John Parker had ever said with all the fancy words he had ever used and never meant in his life. Common ground. A place to make their stand. Home.

She smiled at Michael and her smile did not fade the rest of the day. Not when she met John's lovely wife-to-be or when she accepted a check on behalf of the Parker family to help with the rebuilding of High Plains.

When John had gone and Avery's parents had arrived, she excused herself and went back to the cottages. Michael had asked her to stay, but she didn't feel right about that. She knew he would do the right thing and felt that the last thing Avery and her parents needed was an outsider listening in. Michael had insisted that she was not an outsider, but she felt that, for now at least, she still was. She hadn't added that—*for now*—when she had talked to Michael, but the next day when Michael called her to say he needed her help in picking out something special, she got the idea he was ready to make her nonoutsider status official.

Chapter Seventeen

"I want them all." Avery looked up from a huddle of puppies in the middle of the floor in Lexi Harmon's makeshift animal shelter.

"I told you I needed help picking one out. She's going to want every animal she sees." He chuckled at the picture the kid made with the dogs all vying for her attention and her trying not to leave any one of them out. "And I don't have a clue."

"Tell me about it," Heather grumbled, then, catching herself, winced and laughed at her own lousy attitude. "That is—"

"Don't sweat it," he told her, keeping to himself that just being around her had him sweating enough for the both of them. He'd professed his love and she'd said she loved him, but they hadn't really talked yet about what that meant. If only she would give him some kind of sign.

"Every animal here is healthy." Lexi bent to retrieve one puppy and then another. With them wriggling in her arms, she headed toward the row of kennels lining the floor. "I've checked them all out personally. Any one of them would make a wonderful pet for Avery."

"I don't know. I want something small and sweet and fluffy like…" Avery swung her gaze around. Her face lit up. She pointed. "Like him!"

"Colt?" Lexi stood bolt upright. The puppies in her arms squirmed and licked. She seemed oblivious to anything in the room except her ex-husband, standing in the doorway in his uniform with a small bundle of fur cupped in one hand.

"Is that your kitten?" Avery jabbed her finger tentatively toward the young gray-and-white, tiger-stripe cat.

Colt tore his gaze away from Lexi long enough to look down and scowl. "I found it huddled in a storm drain." He held it out to Lexi. "And I knew just where to bring it."

Michael looked at the two people he had always felt still belonged together. Though he had not officiated at their wedding in the Old Town Hall or counseled them two years ago when their marriage fell apart, Lexi had recently asked him to try to get through to Colt, to try to make the rugged, serious and mostly silent man open up.

Michael had not had any success with that. Seeing the two of them here together now, he wondered if he had simply been the wrong person for the job.

"Can I hold it?" Avery approached the kitten with caution.

"Sure." Colt transferred the animal to Avery by letting it roll gently from his large hand into the girl's arms.

"Hello, there," Avery whispered. "Would you like to come home with me?"

Michael knew in that instant that Avery had found her pet. He looked at Heather, who met his gaze with her eyes slightly misty as she mouthed the word that had all but sealed the deal for him, as well. "Home."

The kitten mewed.

"Aww." Avery and Heather both let out a gooey-girly sound that Michael realized he had better get used to if he was going to have a teenager and a kitten—and maybe a girlfriend? Wife? Softball teammate?—underfoot.

"Thank you for bringing the kitten in." Lexi turned her back to put back the puppies Avery had been playing with.

Colt dropped his gaze to the floor, then nodded his head. "Yeah, well…"

"I'd like to thank you, too, Officer Ridgeway." Heather almost put her hand out, either thinking she would give the man's arm a squeeze or that she would be able to shake his hand. Then she seemed to realize he wasn't the type who appreciated that kind of overture from a woman he didn't know well, so she folded her arms and offered him a warm smile instead. "For our talk the other day."

"Talk?" That got Lexi's attention. The metal kennel door shut with a rattle. She stood and spun around. "You two have been...talking?"

"I was trying to help with the investigation surrounding Kasey," Heather volunteered. "And during the course of that, Officer Ridgeway offered me a little... heartfelt advice."

"Colt?" As soon as the cry of disbelief left her lips, Lexi clapped her hand over her mouth.

Michael didn't know whether to chuckle or cringe. He settled for prying. "He did *what?*"

Heather put her hand on Michael's cheek. "He just pointed out that a certain old friend of mine didn't look at me the way a man looks at a woman he wants as one of his good ol' pals."

"Ah." Was that his sign? He thought maybe it was. Michael nodded and decided he could test both Heather's interest and nudge Colt and Lexi along with a few well-placed conclusions. "So Colt pointed out to you that when two people have real feelings for each other, it's hard to hide it."

Heather gave him a curious look.

"And when a person who cares about those people sees that look in those people's eyes, then it's not out of place for that person to say or do something to try to help those people deal with those feelings they are trying to hide but everyone else can see?"

Colt cleared his throat.

Lexi fiddled with her long brown hair.

"Can I have him…or her?" Avery asked without taking her eyes from the purring cat.

"I'll give the little one a quick health check and let you know if he or…" Lexi practically nabbed the kitten, raised it up, peered in close then corrected herself. "If *she* is well enough to go home with you now. Excuse me."

She didn't leave, just took a step backward.

"I'd better go, too." Colt shifted his feet but did not actually take a single step to leave, either.

"Before either of you get away," Michael spoke up, unwilling to let this opportunity slip by to bring this couple together to deal with their feelings. "I noticed that both of you came to the dedication for the rebuilding of the Old Town Hall and I wonder if you'd consider giving some time to the committee overseeing that work?"

He said it all in one breath, fearing that any break would give them a chance to say no before he got the question out. In fact, not wanting to give them the chance to say no at all, he pressed on. "I mean, the two of you are both so much a part of High Plains and, if I'm not mistaken, you have some personal history with the Old Town Hall, don't you?"

"Uh-huh," Lexi said, cradling Avery's kitten close.

"Yeah." Colt nodded, his eyes straight ahead.

"Great!" Michael clapped his hands together and before they knew what had hit them concluded, "I'll be sure you get the notices on when we meet. You both have so much to offer…to the project, of course."

They both muttered something and ducked out of the room, each in opposite directions.

Avery chased after Lexi. "Can I stay with her while you check her over? I don't want her to be scared without me."

"So it begins," Michael observed.

"So *what* begins?" Heather tilted her head to one side and narrowed her beautiful eyes at him. "You were not just talking about the kitten. You're up to something, Reverend Garrison."

"Up to? Ministers do not get *up to* anything. Ministers go about God's business."

"God's business? And what exactly is God's business in this case, Michael?"

"The same thing it always is, Heather. Love."

"I might argue there's a difference in doing God's work and doing a little light matchmaking." She started to say something more, but he didn't give her the chance.

"Then I'd argue right back that love, the real kind of love that endures all things, the kind that is based in the love that God first had for us, sometimes needs a little something to make the two imperfect human beings realize just what they have and how much they can build on it."

"There you go, talking in riddles, Michael." She shook her head. "Trying to sound things out to make sure everything is just right before you make your move. Maybe, finally, you should just—"

"Marry me."

"Marry? What? Michael! We haven't even gone out on a date!"

"Is that a no?"

"No. I mean, no, that's not…" She shut her eyes, clearly flustered. "I love you. But marriage? It's so… We've only…"

Before she could get out another word, he kissed her the way he had always wanted to kiss her. When the kiss ended her held her close and whispered, "Say yes, Heather."

Her eyes wide and her cheeks pink, she

wet her lips and murmured, "Michael, I've only been in town a few—"

Aware that they didn't have long before Lexi and Avery came back, he grazed his lips over hers again. Lightly first then more insistently. He had waited so long to hold her like this, to kiss her, to make her a part of his family forever. He didn't want to put off hearing her answer another minute. "Say yes."

Her eyes gazed deeply into his at last. She chewed her lower lip for only a moment before she smiled. "I love you, Michael Garrison, and I'd be proud to change my name to yours. Yes."

With that he kissed her again as a man who loved her first as a friend, then as a woman and always as a mate who would love him and the Lord the rest of their days.

* * * * *

tell him. Have you known people like
this? Why do you think that happens?

4. Have you ever volunteered to help in
the aftermath of a crisis? Do you think
it made a change in your own life, not
just in the lives of those you helped?

5. Have you ever dealt with a severe
weather situation before? What happened, and how did you get through it?

6. Avery was a kid who needed a lot of
love and didn't seem to know how to
ask for it. Do you think there are more
young people like Avery now or do you
think it's always hard to ask for love?

7. Michael believed that when we get
involved in something bigger than ourselves, it challenges us to grow to be
equal to the task. Do you believe that?
Can you think of examples of things
you have gotten involved with that
have challenged you to grow?

8. Michael justified not telling Avery about staying on in High Plains because he thought it was her parents' responsibility. Do you agree with this decision? Why or why not?

9. Michael had to confront the idea that doing something in God's time did not always mean waiting but sometimes meant taking immediate action. Do you think that is true?

10. The only time Heather could face the pain she knew she'd feel going into the sanctuary where she had been jilted was when she had to do it to help Avery. Have you ever had a time when, in order to help another person, you had to face a fear and overcome it?

11. Did your parents ever disappoint you, as Avery's did her? Were you able to get past it and have a good relationship? How?

12. What are some ways your community can band together in good times, as High Plains banded together in times of trouble?

13. Michael and Heather realized they loved each other and that they wanted to marry after only a month of being together again. What makes you believe that they will have a successful marriage?

14. What are some ways you think that Heather and Michael can make sure Avery feels at home with them after their marriage?

15. Which character are you hoping will find love in the next four AFTER THE STORM books?

Turn the page for a sneak preview of
REKINDLED HEARTS,
by Brenda Minton,
the next exciting book in the
AFTER THE STORM *series,*
available in September from
Steeple Hill.

Lexi Harmon stood in the entryway of her house, knowing that she shouldn't be there. She should be back in the basement, where she'd gone minutes ago, after she had heard the tornado siren. But her heart wouldn't let her go to the basement, not until she knew if Colt was safe. She'd watched his police car pass earlier.

She knew he would risk his life to save everyone else. He was all about saving other people. If only he had put that same care into their marriage, rather than saying he loved her too much to make it work.

He had divorced her to save her from heartache.

Whatever.

She knew that he had divorced her to save

himself. He didn't want to live his life worrying about her, worrying about what would happen to her if something happened to him. He had divorced her because he hadn't been able to deal with the death of Gavin Jones, a deputy whom Colt hadn't been able to reach in time to save.

As mad as he made her, Lexi's heart still ached when she thought of Colt, of loving him and losing him. She closed her eyes and leaned against the cool glass of the window.

She prayed he would be safe. She couldn't see him out there and she wanted to see him. This felt too much like their marriage, when she had prayed every night that he would come home safe. And one night, a few months after Gavin's death, he hadn't called to let her know he would be late.

He had found her on the couch, crying, afraid that he wasn't coming back. That night had been the final straw for them both.

Now he was out there again. And she was afraid. Again.

It had to be bad. Debris littered her yard—things that hadn't come from her neighborhood. Her power was out and the house was silent. No news on the radio, no hum of the fridge. Silence, other than the howl of the wind picking up again, and rain pelting the windows and metal roof.

"Please, God, keep him safe. Keep our town safe." The wood door shuddered and heaved as the wind ripped across the Kansas plains.

She should go to the basement.

As she turned away from the door, it blew open. And there he was, bloody and heaving as he carried their dog into the house. His dog. Chico had been hers, but after the divorce, he'd picked Colt.

The dog had broken her heart, too. Each time she'd taken him home from Colt's house, the dog had gone back to Colt.

"Colt." She froze for a second and then came to life again, because the house shook and the wind outside had changed. It wasn't blowing straight at the house the way it had. Windows on all sides seemed to be taking a beating from wind and rain, leaves sticking to the glass.

"Get to the basement." Colt's blond hair was rain-soaked and plastered to his head. A streak of blood marked his cheek. "Lexi, go!"

She ran down the hall to the door that led to the basement. She opened it and motioned him down. Before she could go, she needed supplies. She needed something for him, or the dog, whichever one was injured. Her clinic was on the lot next to the house. She couldn't make it over there, not in this storm.

"Lexi, get down here now."

"I'm coming."

She grabbed a few things from the kitchen counter and ran down the stairs, slamming the door behind her. She held the rail and took careful steps in the darkened basement, glad to see a sliver of light from the small window and then the bright beam of a flashlight Colt had found.

"I'm here, in the corner." Colt's voice, soft and firm. He never panicked.

Lexi bit down on her lip, listening to the crash and splinter of trees and the wind slamming her house. Her heart pounded painfully in her chest and she didn't want this to happen, not this, not now.

Not when she was finally starting to get it together again. Total destruction was a perfect marriage crumbling into a nightmare of silence and loneliness. This nightmare she couldn't take, not the town crumbling around her.

What was God thinking? Did He know she had been at the end of her faith rope and she was just beginning to climb back up?

She dug in the bag and Colt moved closer. He grimaced and held his left arm close to his chest with his right hand.

"Are you okay?"

He smiled, like it didn't matter. "Take care of Chico. I'm fine."

A loud crash above them and the shatter of glass. She shuddered and paused, waiting to see if everything would collapse in on them. When the world calmed for a minute, she looked at Colt again, at the arm he held to his side.

"Of course you're fine." She touched his

arm and he flinched. His face was bruised, as well. "What happened out there?"

Tight lines of pain around his mouth. "We're taking a direct hit. I need to make sure the two of you are okay and get back out there."

"Not until I make sure you're okay. You look like you were in a car accident."

"It was nothing like that. A limb hit my arm." He wouldn't tell her more. She knew he didn't want her to picture what had happened out there. What was still happening. But she could hear it.

A huge crash above them. Lexi jumped, tingles sliding up her arms and through her scalp. She closed her eyes and waited.

"Lexi, it's okay." Colt's voice, steady and calm.

She opened her eyes and he was watching her.

"Of course it is." She tried to smile but she couldn't, not with the storm raging outside her home and inside her heart, fear tangling with adrenaline. "The town falling in around us is okay."

"We're safe."

She nodded, not really believing it. She'd watched the news all morning, national coverage of storms ripping across Kansas, taking lives, taking homes and dreams. It had been a huge supercell that started in the southwest and was moving northeast, across their state. She had prayed it would stop, that it would turn away from them.

But upstairs the wind was pounding her house, and through the narrow basement window she could see debris scooting across her lawn. A crash vibrated through the house and she trembled. A quick glance at the window, and this time she saw only tree limbs against the glass.

The door slammed. Wind wailed outside, roaring like a train about to come off the tracks. More glass shattering. And then the windows in the basement. Lexi ducked as a pipe in the basement ceiling fell.

It was an old house, and the upstairs hardwood floor and underlying support beams were the ceiling for the basement. Pipes and electrical wires crisscrossed the big, open room, making it not the safest place to be in a tornado. She preferred the storage room in the far corner of the basement.

Then the house above them splintered and crackled. "Run to the laundry room," Colt ordered.

Colt's voice was drowned by the roaring wind. He reached them, grabbing the dog and pushing behind her. A board splintered and fell. Lexi tried to duck, but the board hit the arm she lifted to shield herself and then it hit her head.

Crashing and roaring filled her ears and the world tilted. Colt was behind her, pushing her forward.

"Don't fall, Lexi. Keep moving."

"I can't." She was dizzy, and her eyes clouded for a second. Her legs buckled and she felt Colt's arm against hers. Her ears popped and her lungs heaved for air. "I can't."

"Five more steps. You can." He shoved with his shoulder and they were in the storage room, the door slamming behind him. The building quaked around them.

A house over one hundred years old, and today it gave up. Lexi cried because the house had history. The house had stood the test of time.

It was the one thing in her life that had been sturdy and unwavering. It had a history that she had wanted, of families growing up and growing old together. As she ran to the far corner of the room, she knew the house was falling in around them.

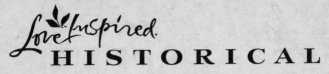

HISTORICAL

INSPIRATIONAL HISTORICAL ROMANCE

Engaging stories of romance,
adventure and faith,
these novels are set in
various historical periods
from biblical times
to World War II.

NOW AVAILABLE!

Steeple
Hill®

For exciting stories that reflect traditional values,
visit:
www.SteepleHill.com

QUESTIONS FOR DISCUSSION

1. Heather seemed more able to forgive being jilted by her young fiancé than she was able to get over feeling betrayed by Michael, her friend. Have you ever been betrayed by a friend? Do you think it is harder to move on from that than from a romantic breakup?

2. Heather had a deep emotional connection to her hometown, and seeing it again was the beginning of breaking down her defenses. Is there a place that you have not been in a long time that you wish you could visit again? Do you think returning to a place with special connections can have life-changing effects?

3. Michael seemed to be very good at stepping into crises and caring for his community and congregation, but he was often clueless about his personal life and what his loved ones were really trying to

Dear Reader,

When asked to participate in the AFTER THE STORM series, I jumped at the chance to work with this wonderful group of writers to tell the story of the good people of High Plains, Kansas. Like many of the other authors, I have plenty of first-hand experience with tornadoes, having lived in "Tornado Alley" (Enid, Stillwater, Oklahoma City, Oklahoma, and Kansas City, Missouri). I grew up with parents who had tremendous faith and taught us to respect the storms and be smart about them—something I confess I've forgotten more than once—and to trust in the Lord. Time and again I've watched as people have relied on faith for comfort in the aftermath of these storms, and I drew on that in telling the story of Michael and Heather.

Annie Jones